The Garden of Earthly Delights turns to Hell in a single flash

The massive fist impacted on Bolan's temple, sending him sprawling. The enemy's howl drowned the ringing in his ears.

Bolan collided with the desk, rebounded, fought to regain his balance. But the monster man was on top of him, driving him back into the desk.

His left arm, pinned by the bear-hugging giant, could not reach the Beretta. The vicelike hold was crushing the life from Bolan's body, sending racking spasms of pain up his spine.

Blood roared in his ears.

He recognized the warning signs of impending blackout.

He recognized the warning signs of death.

'Millions of Americans are turning to the incomparable Mack Bolan. Required reading in Washington policymaking circles!"
—*Chicago Sun-Times*

D0448726

Also available from Gold Eagle Books,
publishers of the Executioner Series:

Mack Bolan's
ABLE TEAM

Mack Bolan's
PHOENIX FORCE

MACK

THE EXECUTIONER 60

BOLAN

Sold for Slaughter

A GOLD EAGLE BOOK FROM

TORONTO • NEW YORK • LONDON • PARIS
AMSTERDAM • STOCKHOLM • HAMBURG
ATHENS • MILAN • TOKYO • SYDNEY

First edition December 1983

ISBN 0-373-61060-2

Special thanks and acknowledgment to
Mike Newton for his contributions to this work.

Printed in Canada

Better an end with horrors than horrors without an end.
> —*Macedonian peasant slogan during the Ilenden Uprising against the empire of the Turks*

The seeker of truth is a student of death.
> —*Mack Bolan*

Dedicated to the 269 passengers
of KAL Flight 007. We shall not forget them.

PROLOGUE

After three days, Mack Bolan was prepared to give up hope. He knew the odds against survival, and he knew that death was virtually certain. And while that knowledge ripped at his guts, there was nothing he could do.

A missing agent was a fellow soldier's primal fear. Sudden death was preferable to the nagging doubts and open-ended questions that a disappearance left behind. Bolan knew the consequences of falling into savage hands, and he wished the hostage, if nothing else, a quick, clean kill.

Death could be a blessing, sweet release.

Bolan remembered the tortured sound of helpless, hopeless screaming, a sound he had heard many times before, and it sickened him, provoked a tremor of the soul. The enemy continually found new methods of torture, but the result was always the same—pain.

Silently, the soldier cursed his endless war.

Combatants knew the game and took their chances, but when it came down to basics there were no expendable allies. If Bolan's bloody war had taught him any single lesson, it was that everybody counts. That truth—the fundamental worth of human life and dignity—was at the heart of every Mack Bolan action.

Undeniably, there were practical considerations. A hostage-taking was potentially disastrous for the Stony Man program. Any leak of information, a revelation under torture, could disrupt the mission irreversibly. There were contingencies and options if the hostage could be found in time, before the will was broken.

If the agent could be reached without exposing the project.

If. . . .

Bolan was concerned at present with the human factor—the flesh-and-blood investment—rather than the tactical. He would spare no effort to save the hostage—or to hand out final, fiery retribution on the enemy.

But first, he had to find a handle on the situation, something to point him in the right direction. Somehow, somewhere, he knew there had to be a way around the screen of silence. A way inside the problem.

Bolan waited and spent the anxious hours in a constant state of combat readiness, hoping for some word out of Wonderland on the Potomac. When the call came, early on the fourth day, he listened to the disembodied voice of Hal Brognola.

"We've found her, Striker. She's alive."

Bolan heard him out and felt the pieces falling into place around him, giving him the angle that he needed. By the time Brognola broke the telephone link, Bolan had both target and ETA confirmed.

The waiting was all over now.

He would return to the hellgrounds with a vengeance now, carrying his endless war to the enemy doorstep. If he found the hostage less than safe and whole, there would be hellfire enough to go around for everyone concerned.

Bolan began the Bolan Effect.

1

The buyer from Chicago parked his Maserati between two carbon-copy Continentals, backing in to give himself an easy exit. All along the white picket fence, a line of flashy vehicles were parked, some of them with chauffeurs in attendance. The tall man could feel enemy eyes upon him as he left his sportster.

He had seen their roadside defenses, had noted sentries mounted and on foot and closed-circuit cameras stationed every hundred yards along the road to this bogus farm, which concealed a special marketplace. It was impossible to reach the marketplace unnoticed, unidentified, without passing inspection.

A ceiling of gunmetal clouds obscured the sky; lightning danced over Kansas City. The buyer closed his rain jacket and moved across the parking area with brisk strides. He did not expect a challenge here, but the pistol's weight beneath his arm was reassuring.

On unfamiliar ground, he knew it paid to take precautions.

The farm, run by Benny Battaglia, would pass a casual inspection from the ground or air, and it would take a suicide commando to penetrate the carefully prepared camouflage. House, barn and the other clustered outbuildings all presented a serene, pastoral image to the uninitiated.

Benny Battaglia was relatively new to Kansas, even newer to the farming life. He was a city boy in exile, routed from St. Louis by an antivice crusade that closed his thriving chain of "escort services" and left him facing indictment. The flight had cost him money and prestige, but he was still a pimp at heart, addicted to the easy life of trafficking in human degradation. With some ready capital and willing contacts, he had found the makings of another empire in the heartland.

The buyer reached his destination and a sentry, clad in faded denims, nodded and passed him on into the barn. A blast of hot air enveloped the big man as he entered.

The inside of the marketplace took his breath away.

The cavernous interior had been converted into something from a pornographic fairy tale. Rows of stalls designed for dairy cattle held a different kind of living merchandise on display for shoppers drifting up and down the aisles. Overhead, the loft had been converted into an observation deck, and spotters armed with automatic rifles kept watchful eyes on the trading floor.

The buyer marked the gunners, mentally recording ranges and angles, but he concentrated on the holding pens. Each contained a pair of young, attractive women. Quickly surveying all the pens, he noticed that the women represented every race and many nationalities. It was a skin display of infinite variety, but every face revealed the same drugged apathy. All the women were naked under the bright fluorescent lights, but each appeared oblivious to scrutiny from men in business suits who moved among them, pausing here and there to comment.

The buyer saw Battaglia approaching, and he moved to greet the master of the marketplace. He took the hand that Benny offered, shook it and suppressed a shudder at the slaver's slimy touch. Benny's smile was cautious, the expression of a crocodile assessing prey.

"Hey, Chicago. Glad you could make it down." Battaglia hesitated, then added, "Guess I didn't catch the name."

The buyer passed a business card. Benny took it and read the single word on it.

Omega.

The final letter of the Greek alphabet.

The end.

Battaglia slowly reversed the business card,

and found an ace of spades printed on the flip side. The color left his cheeks as he stared at the card. It took a moment for the mobster to regain his voice. "It's been a long time since I saw one of these."

Chicago offered him a frosty smile. "We didn't all go down with Pat and Mike," he said.

"I see."

Battaglia knew that the black ace was a death card and the symbol of the Mafia's elite gestapo. Hand-selected by the legendary Talifero brothers, Pat and Mike, the Aces were a breed apart, inspiring fear among the ranks of the Cosa Nostra. Answering directly to *La Commissióne*, they could hit a boss without specific orders should the need arise, and they had exercised that ultimate prerogative on more than one occasion.

But the Aces had become endangered species. A crazy Green Beret—that Bolan bastard—had declared a private holy war against the brotherhood, and the syndicate's elite exterminators found themselves on the defensive. Pat and Mike had fallen in the Bolan blitz, their cadres decimated, those remaining scattered to the winds. Rumors of survivors had circulated through the underworld, but Battaglia had never planned on meeting an Ace in person.

The slaver tried to grin. "I guess this ain't no ordinary shopping trip," he said.

"Nothing's ordinary around here, Benny."

"Yeah... well, uh... what can I do for you, Omega?"

"Let me have the tour. I'd like to see your operation."

A ripple of concern registered in Battaglia's narrow eyes.

The Black Ace fell in beside Battaglia, keeping pace along the nearest line of stalls. He listened to the nervous monologue without absorbing any of it; he was looking at the women, scanning faces. In their present state, the youthful bodies were pathetic rather than provocative. Other patrons, however, did not share his view; Omega gathered from the scraps of conversation overheard in passing that they liked the show immensely.

The Ace was looking for a special woman, one face in particular.

Battaglia showed him at least half the human inventory before he found her, sharing quarters with an Oriental captive in a corner stall. Omega knew her at a glance. The heavy shadowing around her eyes, her dark hair all tangled did not obscure her classic profile.

He would have known her anywhere.

Omega lingered by the railing, looking at the seated woman. Battaglia continued on a few more steps before realizing he was all alone and talking to himself. The slaver doubled back to join the Ace, his smile confident, assertive. Once again he was the master salesman in a seller's market, moving in to close the deal.

"See something there you like?"

Omega indicated his selection with a nod. "Right here," he said.

Battaglia looked at the Black Ace's choice, and something clicked behind his oval face. The air of confidence, so newly found, was swiftly dissipating. "I can show you something better if you're really in the market," he muttered.

"No," the Ace replied. "I came for her."

The pimp was plainly worried. "I, uh, guess I don't follow you. . . ."

"I guess you're not supposed to, Benny."

Confusion moved up an octave to outright anxiety. Battaglia was picking up vibrations that he seriously did not like. "She's trouble," he informed Omega. "All the way."

The Ace regarded him in silence, his attitude forcing elaboration.

"Listen, she was asking questions, sniffing around. I could have wasted her, but I decided to break even on the deal."

Omega shook his head. "Clumsy, Ben. You been thinking with your prick."

Battaglia stiffened, color flooding back into his cheeks. "Now, wait a second there—"

"You haven't got a second, guy. It's now or never."

Battaglia wanted to reply but found no words.

"It's *family* business, Benny," the buyer said. "You don't need to know."

Battaglia's caution now jostled with anger, which momentarily won out. "Is that right? She was running down her act on *my* turf, remember. Seems to me I've got a vested interest."

"Ever stop to figure *why* she picked your turf?" the Ace asked. "Who's behind it, anyway?"

"I've got a major operation here," Battaglia blustered. "The Feds—"

"Could have bagged you in St. Louis, Benny. Off the record, people wonder why they didn't."

"People? What people?"

"Well, if you have to ask...."

The anger faltered in Battaglia, fell away, and fear was in the saddle now. "You're kidding, right?"

"You've got a lot of friends, Battaglia, but the wind is shifting. It could blow your house down."

"You say."

"Fair enough." The Ace was brushing past him, moving toward the exit. "See you in the papers."

"Hey...well, Jesus, *wait* a second, will ya?"

Omega hesitated, then swiveled back to face Battaglia.

"I'll need your full cooperation, starting now," he said.

"Okay, okay . . . ."

"The girl," Omega said. "She comes with me."

Battaglia stood silently as if arguing with himself, then spoke at last. "What else?"

"That's it—for now." The Ace checked his wristwatch. "I'm working on a deadline here. They want her back in Chicago tonight."

"Yeah, great." The slaver cleared his throat and tried to sound cooperative. "Let me scare up a dress or something for her."

"Never mind."

The Ace was shrugging off his rain jacket, moving past Battaglia and then on inside the holding pen. He got the woman on her feet. She moaned as he supported her, with an arm around her slender waist, his free hand guiding naked arms into the jacket sleeves. The rain jacket bottomed out at the very top of her bare thighs, but it was all he had to offer and the Ace was feeling pressed for time. He could feel Battaglia's nervousness; waves of doubt were radiating from the guy.

Omega propped the woman against the railing of the holding pen, and for a fractured second she connected with his gaze. Recognition flickered in her eyes beneath the drooping lids. Then she lost eye contact, wobbling as she tried to stay on her feet. He steered her through the open gate and out to where Battaglia was waiting, an uneasy frown carving furrows in his swarthy face.

The slaver was having second thoughts, working up the nerve to ask another question. Omega saw it coming and took the opportunity to unbutton his sports jacket, making the holstered automatic more accessible. "I guess I'd better make a call," the slaver said, thinking out loud.

"Fine. You got the number there?"

"I know some people in Chicago, sure."

"Get on it, then. Tell them I'll be late because you can't make up your mind."

Battaglia stiffened, clenched his fists until the knuckles whitened. Silent argument still raged in his head, and the strain was showing in his attitude and posture. "Never mind," he spat. "You'd better go."

Omega scowled as he led the woman past her former captor, forcing him to step aside. Moving briskly, almost dragging her along, the Ace was closing on the exit when he caught a glimpse of Benny from the corner of his eye. The slaver was gesturing, summoning a gunner from the sidelines. He saw them huddle and watched the hood dash away—to find a telephone, no doubt.

The sentry at the door let them pass, and in a heartbeat they had cleared the barn. The woman shivered as the chill attacked her exposed thighs.

Omega pulled her close against him and kept her moving across the open parking lot. On his flank, a pair of chauffeurs lounging up against a silver Rolls were staring at the woman and whispering. Knowing laughter followed them until they reached the Maserati.

He was helping her into the Maserati's starboard bucket seat when Benny Battaglia, shouting, erupted from the barn with guns in tow. Omega tucked the woman in, closed her door and took his pistol from its sling before he turned and moved away from the car to face the challenge.

His weapon was the Beretta 93-R, equipped with special silencer. Fifteen 9mm steel-jackets filled the magazine in staggered-box configuration, with a sixteenth ready in the firing chamber. The gun was metallurgically altered; thus, the steel jackets did not cause excess wear, reducing accuracy to the level of an "area-type" weapon. On the contrary, the steel-jackets increased chamber pressures to release greater energy and muzzle velocity, hence accuracy. The 93-R was capable of double-action semi-automatic fire, or three-round bursts in fully automatic mode, dispensing death at a cyclic rate of 110 rounds per minute. A genuine machine pistol, the 93-R was, in a marksman's hands, deadly to ranges of 100 yards and more.

Battaglia and his troops were less than fifty yards away.

Omega pivoted, the pistol coming up and out to full extension, locking onto target. Down-range, half a dozen men were clustered at the entrance to the barn. Battaglia was already moving closer. The slaver had found himself a weapon, and was leveling it in the Ace's direction.

Omega tripped the fire-selector switch and squeezed the trigger, rattling off a triple-punch in autofire. Battaglia staggered, breaking stride. His expensive blazer ripped with the stunning impact. Blood spurted from him in a crimson spray.

Behind Battaglia, the gunners were reacting like experienced professionals, unlimbering their weapons and bringing them to bear upon the human target. In another instant they would have him.

Omega squeezed the trigger twice, the muzzle sweeping back and forth. The hollow men were sent diving, sprawling, scattering, their first rounds going high and wild.

The Ace moved out. He went into a shoulder roll across the Maserati's hood and came to earth again beside the driver's door. Another beat and he was at the wheel, firing up the power and open-throttling away before the scattered gunners could recover.

Ahead of him, a chauffeur interposed himself between Omega and the open road. The guy's

.45 was up and bucking, heavy slugs impacting on the Maserati's windshield, transforming it to broken crystal. Navigating with his sixth sense, the Ace let his charger drift, acquiring a collision course.

The gunner turned to run, but it was far too late. The bumper took him low and hard, rolling him up across the sloping hood; an elbow hit the windshield, safety glass turned to pebbles, and the guy was gone, an airborne sack of broken bones.

Omega gained the drive, accelerator on the floor, powering away. Behind him, a shotgun roared and pellets raked the Maserati's flank. Another moment, and they flashed around a curve, out of range—but not out of mortal danger.

2

Mack Bolan—the "Chicago Ace"—was used to living on the edge. A soldier since his teens, he knew the risks of battle, and he knew a hundred ways to mitigate those risks. The military had taught him martial arts, the warrior's trade, and he had picked up some unique skills along the hellfire trail. One skill, the fine art of role camouflage, had served him well in many of his campaigns—from the jungles of Southeast Asia to another kind of jungle stateside.

In Vietnam, the Executioner had been a specialist at infiltration and assassination. Cut off behind enemy lines, he had often used role camouflage to save himself from almost certain death or capture. Crouching in a rice paddy, clad in black pajamas and a coolie hat, he had watched a Vietcong procession pass within seventy-five yards of his exposed position. Charlie had been searching for a tall American, and he was not looking for an enemy dressed in peasant garb.

When his Asian war had been abbreviated,

shifted to another battlefront, the soldier found a chance to hone his skills.

With arrogance derived from years of uncontested power and dominion, *mafiosi* had come to expect their employees and potential victims to behave in certain ways. Those expectations had permitted Bolan to employ certain skills against the enemy with great success. From California to Manhattan, he had actually infiltrated "families," bringing fiery retribution to them from within. Finally, his impersonation of Omega, a lethal Black Ace of Bolan's own invention, had resulted in eradication of the Mafia's elite gestapo.

He had brought their rotten house down, but several real Aces had escaped his wrath. However, they were blamed for much of Bolan's damage, were feared and hated even by their brother mobsters, hunted through the shaken underworld and finally forgotten when their threat was dissipated.

But a single Ace, obviously, remained. Omega was available for special missions.

It had been a risky proposition, infiltrating Ben Battaglia's stronghold. Bolan had assessed the odds, considered going in for blood and finally dismissed the frontal blitz as foolish. There were hostages to be considered; his line of fire might be all-inclusive. So he went in cold. A soft probe—no flames.

And it had worked—to a point. Battaglia's isolation from the mainstream of syndicate activity, his insecurity had made the pimp an easy mark at first. But underneath the surface, a suspicion born of long experience with Mafia betrayal politics had alerted him to Bolan's double cross. There had been a trace of steel inside the slaver. Not enough to make him bullet-proof, however.

Role camouflage had served its purpose for Bolan once more. Now he would need a different set of skills to get away from the marketplace alive.

His passenger was groggy. The sound of gunfire and the cold air rushing through the shattered windshield helped only a little to fight the drugs that dulled her senses. She was sitting up, looking around, dazedly seeking recognition of her new surroundings. "Where are you taking me?"

"We're going home," he told her.

But first they had to make it out of Ben Battaglia's net alive. The master pimp was dead, but he had punched the panic button and the trap was closing.

Up ahead, a pair of mounted spotters had appeared along the fence, galloping to meet the Maserati. Each spotter was carrying an automatic carbine, lining up the target and squeezing off initial probing rounds.

Bolan reached beneath the driver's seat and sprang the mini-Uzi from its hidden rigging. Specially designed to mingle firepower with concealability, the submachine gun measured only fourteen inches in length. Its magazine held thirty-two 9mm parabellum rounds. At any reasonable range it was a man-shredder, firing at a cyclic rate of 750 rounds per minute.

Rifle slugs tore the air around the Maserati, the gunners finding range and elevation. A bullet whispered between the soldier and his passenger, exploding through the back window. At Bolan's side, the woman reacted on instinct, diving for cover underneath the dash. Bolan thrust the Uzi through his open windshield.

A mounted figure drifted into range above his open sights, the rifle up and bucking. Bolan stroked the trigger, riding out the recoil, empty casings clattering along the dashboard. He saw the horse stumble, fall, its rider catapulting from the saddle. Close behind him, another rider was taken by surprise. He dropped his weapon, wrestled with the reins—and plowed his animal directly into that of his companion.

Bolan helped him in his fall with a short, precision burst. He had an image of the rider's face and chest exploding into bloody fragments, then the twisting, writhing heap of man and animal dwindled in his rearview mirror and faded fast.

The hounds would be in hot pursuit by now,

and they would have the exit closed against him. They were in the pincers, but with planning and a little luck....

A Lincoln made the curve behind him, with a pair of matching Cadillacs in tow. There were seats for twenty soldiers if they crowded in.

There were enough guncocks to do the job, but they had to catch him first. It was over when the final body fell, and not before.

A last lazy turn, and then the drive ran arrow-straight along its final quarter mile. Bolan saw the gatehouse. Foot soldiers were milling all around it, forming a ragged skirmish line. The wrought-iron gates were shut and chained together, but Bolan kept the hammer down and held the Maserati steady on her course.

He had foreseen the possibility of a withdrawal under fire and prepared himself for it. A savvy warrior always kept his flank protected, and Bolan was an expert at survival in the hell-grounds.

He found a button underneath the dash and pressed it, flashing a silent signal ahead of him. The message was received, registered, and out beyond the range of human eyes a trigger mechanism was activated by remote control. Bolan was waiting, counting down to impact, when a fiery comet fell upon the gatehouse, detonating in an oily ball of flame.

The sentry post disintegrated. Shattered masonry and smoking shrapnel sliced through the ranks of Bolan's enemies. The dead and dying fell together. Orders were forgotten as matters of survival took priority. A single shot was fired at Bolan, then the gunner bolted, sprinting toward safety.

The twisted ruin of Battaglia's gate was swinging in the smoky breeze, its hinges shattered by the blast. Bolan hit the grillwork just off center and felt the Maserati's hood and fenders buckle as he burst through. A heartbeat's hesitation, hellish grinding as the gate was dragged along their flank, and then they made the open highway, running free and clear.

He led the Lincoln and her flankers by about half a minute. They could never overtake his charger on the straightaway, but he had no intention of allowing them to trail him home. He would have to take them out.

In his rearview mirror, Bolan saw the Continental reach the open gate and rumble through, a Caddy close behind. Bolan keyed the dashboard switch a second time, dividing his attention between his tail and the flat Kansas highway stretching out in front of him.

He saw the comet coming, rattling across his track from north to south, homing on the doomsday signal. It was going to be close. The second Cadillac was closing on the gate, her driver taking time to navigate around the smoking bodies.

Caution doomed the wheelman and his passengers. They were at the gate when Bolan's bird impacted on the Caddy's nose, erupting into smoke and flame. In another instant, the gas tank followed in a searing secondary blast, incinerating flesh and twisted steel.

That would hold them for a while; the burning hulk would act as a plug to keep his enemies inside the fence.

The Maserati's radio was tuned to a preselected frequency. Bolan turned it on, cranked the volume up and was rewarded with a ringing silence from the dashboard speakers. He was sending rather than receiving—a Mayday message to friendly, waiting cars.

Brognola would be listening, his force of federal marshals in position around the farm. The ring was closing, and the buyers at Battaglia's auction were about to be presented with a different kind of tab.

The Executioner dismissed them. He knew the women would be cared for when the smoke cleared. In the meantime, there were other battles left to fight, and his opponents were behind him, gaining ground.

The woman was sitting up again, the effort costing her. Bolan pushed her firmly back into her crouch.

"Stay down," he snapped. "We haven't lost them yet."

"Be careful," she replied.

Sleepy as her voice sounded, there was something in her tone that let him know she was not just concerned about herself.

Bolan eased back on his accelerator, heard the engine winding down a notch. The Lincoln's driver saw his chance and surged ahead, riding up against the Maserati's tail before he cut across into the other lane. The tank was pulling beside him, and Bolan felt the hostile eyes upon him, gunners sizing up the opposition.

With a sidelong glance, Bolan saw the power windows dropping and automatic weapons poking into view, muzzles tracking onto target. Bolan felt the numbers falling. He knew that any wrong move would be his last.

He lifted his foot off the gas and simultaneously hit the brake, standing the Maserati on her nose. Before the engine had a chance to stall, he shifted down and cut the steering wheel to port, accelerating again and swinging out to take his enemy on the driver's side.

Ahead of him, the gunners had been surprised. They fired a straggling burst across the sportster's bow, the bullets slicing empty air. They were not prepared for him when he approached them on their blind side. Some of the gunmen were turning, swinging weapons around to greet him, when he brought the curtain down.

Bolan had the mini-Uzi up and was sighting

onto target acquisition as he passed the Lincoln. He could see the driver gaping at him—and he held the submachine gun's trigger down. A dozen feet away, the driver's window shivered, glass dissolving, and the face became a crimson mask, devoid of all humanity.

The Continental started drifting, lifeless hands upon the wheel. Bolan left them to their fate, accelerating away. The Lincoln swerved, lost traction and started rolling. The Cadillac collided with the crashed Lincoln: metal kissed metal.

The Executioner swung the Maserati over on a grassy shoulder and brought her to a halt. In a second he was EVA, feeding a fresh clip into the little stutter gun as he retraced his steps to search the track for enemy survivors.

Four gunmen were scrambling from the disabled Caddy, abandoning the driver who was slumped across the wheel, his face a bloody smear from impact with the windshield.

As Bolan approached, he swung up the Uzi and selected his first target. The burst was short and surgically precise, parabellum manglers blasting a gorilla clean across the Caddy's trunk.

A pair of gunners turned to meet the threat, their weapons still in hand and seeking targets. Bolan hit them with a blazing figure eight, which started at their knees and ended level with their shooting irons, a dozen steel-jackets ripping flesh and fabric into bloody tatters. Both of them died on their feet and fell away in opposite directions, never finding time to trigger any counterfire.

A bullet whistled past Bolan's ear, and he was diving out of range before he heard the shot itself. Flattened on the pavement, he let off another burst, probing for a hot spot and finding it beneath the crew wagon's hood. The car blew, shock wave washing over Bolan. Hungry flames devoured the Cadillac, reaching swiftly to the Lincoln.

He was waiting, ready, when a burning scarecrow burst from cover, reeling out and into open view. Bolan put a single mercy round between the panicked eyes, dropping his final adversary in a twitching heap upon the tarmac.

He put the funeral pyre behind him, slid behind the Maserati's wheel and cranked her up again. He was out of there and running true before he felt the woman watching him.

"Is it over?" she asked.

"For the moment." Bolan dredged up a weary grin and passed it on. "It's good to see you, Smiley."

3

Smiley Dublin in the flesh, every luscious inch of her intact. Bolan had expected worse, much worse.

It had been a while, and seeing Smiley now triggered images of his past.

He remembered the Vegas strike early in his war against the Mafia, when he had first encountered four lovely young performers called the Ranger Girls. They were the hottest act on Glitter Gulch, yet doubled as dynamic agents of the federal Sensitive Operations Group. Smiley was among them, and together with her sisters of the badge—Toby Ranger, Sally Palmer and Georgette Chableu—she had provided welcome aid and comfort to the Bolan war machine. There had been dragons to slay in Vegas, and he was gratified to discover allies there.

The second time their paths had crossed was in Hawaii, where Chinese Communists and *mafiosi* were combining forces in a demonic extortion scheme. It was the Cuban missile crisis reenacted on American terrain, and Smiley was on the inside, working undercover. Between them they had consigned the enemy to cleansing fire and wrestled victory from the Hawaiian battlefield. In the aftermath of battle, they had clung together briefly, sharing tender moments and restoring one another for the wars to come.

Long, bloody miles lay between Hawaii and the plains of Kansas. Perilous miles along the hellfire trail of everlasting war. Lately, Bolan had not dared to hope that they would meet again. He had approached Battaglia's ranch prepared to wreak a brutal vengeance in the woman's name. But, instead, he had brought her out of there alive.

It was a victory to balance out the losses.

He thought of sweet Georgette Chableu. The beautiful Canadian had taken on the Mafia in Motor City and disappeared—like Smiley—in the middle of her covert operation. Bolan had arrived too late to save her, but he had released her body from the degradations of the turkey makers and destroyed the local syndicate in his unbridled rage.

Today, he had arrived in time, and it felt good, damn good. Today had been for Smiley and for the memory of Georgette.

As Bolan ruminated, he sat at the wheel of the Laser Wagon. He was heading east, 450 cubic inches underneath the hood propelling him along the endless prairie highway. Battaglia's farm was history. It was time for Bolan to be thinking of the future.

They were entering Missouri when he felt another presence in the cab. Smiley slid into the seat beside him. The mobile home was self-contained, and she had found the shower and swapped the rain jacket for a jumpsuit out of Bolan's closet. The suit was too large, an almost clownish fit, but Bolan never felt the urge to laugh. In any attire Smiley Dublin was a lot of woman.

"Hi," she greeted him.

The soldier looked her over admiringly, delighted that the old familiar sparkle was returning to her eyes. "Hi, yourself."

"I owe you one."

"Forget it. Ben Battaglia was a running sore. I cauterized it."

"Guess I don't have to ask how you found me."

"Friends keep in touch," Bolan told her. "You were missed."

A silence fell between them. Smiley finally spoke. "I'm glad you're in the picture."

Bolan frowned at the highway. The picture, as painted by Hal Brognola, was an ugly one. Attractive girls and women, ages ranging from fifteen to twenty-five, were disappearing from the Midwest area. Hell, it could be a *national* phenomenon, but interjurisdictional communications left a lot to be desired, and many of the missing had been pegged as runaways, dropouts from society. There were 100,000 people listed as missing every year in America, and usually the disappearing act was easily explained by relatives or creditors. And then there was the *other* kind, those who would still be lost without a trace except for blind coincidence, perhaps the hand of fate.

A private plane with seven passengers, bound for Mexico and points south, had deviated from its flight plan out of Dallas and wrapped itself around some power pylons in a failed attempt to fly beneath the border radar nets. Everyone aboard had been killed on impact or in the searing fire that followed, but autopsies had revealed a wealth of information. The pilot was a veteran border-hopper, with convictions on his sheet for smuggling marijuana and cocaine. His passengers were female, and Texas coroners discovered evidence that all of them had been heavily sedated prior to death.

The Stony Man organization had discovered something else: five of the six had been reported missing from Kansas City and Chicago in the previous six months. And there had been a clincher in the form of registration on the plane; it had been purchased by a small subsidiary of Heartland Produce—a firm originally organized and wholly owned by one Benedetto Battaglia.

Enter Smiley Dublin.

She had penetrated Battaglia's operation as she had the enemy encampment in Hawaii, feeding back a string of promising reports. She had been getting close, but something had gone awry. Smiley vanished, and alarms had started going off in Washington.

Enter Mack Bolan.

And exit Ben Battaglia.

The festering sore had been cauterized, certainly, but the malignancy remained. It would be Bolan's task to search the cancer out, destroy it. To accomplish that, he would require a starting point.

It was debriefing time, a temporary respite from the battlefield. The soldier and the lady were a million miles away from R&R.

In the end, he did not have to ask.

"Battaglia was easy," Smiley said, "or at least I thought he was. He couldn't help believing that I found him irresistible."

Bolan caught a note of self-deprecation in the tone, as if she half expected him to criticize her mode of infiltration. Nothing of the sort had crossed his mind. A soldier—male or female— used the weapons that were made available by nature or design.

"What went wrong?" he asked her.

Smiley flashed a rueful grin and shook her head. "The classic killer: overconfidence. He caught me rifling some files, that's all."

Her faraway expression and Bolan's knowledge of Battaglia and his kind assured the soldier that it would not have been "all," by any means. The slaver would have wanted answers in a hurry, and the questioning had clearly been an ordeal. But Bolan did not have to ask if she had given anything away.

Battaglia's explanation, that he planned to make a profit on his unresponsive hostage rather than to dispose of her quickly, fitted with everything Bolan knew about the guy. His greed had gotten in the way, and it had killed him in the end.

"You were lucky," Bolan told her, thinking aloud.

"Yes," she said. "I was. Battaglia's into everything from running drugs and weapons to illegal aliens, but women are his bread and butter."

"Mainly foreign exports?"

She nodded.

"Ninety-five percent. It's risky with the evidence too close to home."

It all fitted. The border-hopping pilot was headed for South America with new, unwilling conscripts for the brothels there. And from what he had seen inside Battaglia's auction room, half a dozen victims would have been a small transaction. A drop in the cesspool. The slaver's largest customers would be in Asia, Africa, the Middle East, where money earned from oil and heroin was in abundance, aching to be spent.

Battaglia could not have put that all together on his own, the Executioner was certain. He had been a middle-ranker, lacking the resources or prestige to float a major project single-handedly. There had to be a link, a go-between, with larger brains and bankrolls on the other end.

"I need a name," he told the female Fed.

She thought about it for a moment, chewing on her bottom lip in concentration.

"There was one," she said. "I overheard some conversations with a man Battaglia called the Weasel. Never to his face, of course. When they were on the phone, it was just plain Tommy."

Recognition signals started flashing in Bolan's brain. He made the name, and dredged a face out of his mental mug file. The Weasel tag was not uncommon in the underworld, but this one's first name and his link to Ben Battaglia reminded the Executioner of one specific rodent.

He would have to check it out, in any case, and that would mean a trip to Jersey.

"You up to traveling?" he asked.

She watched him for a moment, read the meaning in his tone and smiled. "As ready as I'll ever be."

She had earned the right to come along on this one. She was a pro, and she had made the case her own with blood and sweat and tears. The soldier trusted her implicitly, as much as any other ally, male or female, and he knew she would give her life before she let him down.

The soldier checked his watch and started calculating mileage to St. Louis. Brognola would have their transportation waiting if he called ahead requesting an emergency airlift. It was short notice, but there was no time to lose.

Bolan and Smiley had a date to keep in Jersey.

With a weasel.

4

It was the oldest racket known to man, and from the beginning it had attracted parasites and vultures, preying on the weak and helpless. Women offered or were forced to give their bodies as commodities for many reasons—but the scavengers did not care about the reasons, they were single-minded in pursuit of easy profit. If a pimp could not maintain his "stable" by the force of personality alone, he would resort to other methods—savage beatings, mutilation, even murder if the ultimate example was considered necessary. If willing prostitutes were unavailable, abduction was a viable alternative.

Another generation of reformers coined a name for it: white slavery. The early slavers, circa 1900, representing rival tongs—the Chinese Mafia—engaged in bitter warfare as they shuttled hapless hostages along a secret network spread from San Francisco to Manhattan. A decade later, Congress had responded with the Mann Act. Meant to curb the trade in human flesh, the Act had been used primarily to harass private couples; its impact on the syndicate was negligible.

In the thirties, Charlie "Lucky" Luciano and a score of underlings were tried, convicted and imprisoned for compulsory prostitution, part of Thomas Dewey's war against the New York Mafia. But the racket endured and was passed on to other hands.

Ben Battaglia was an heir to Luciano's legacy—not in power, but in his tendency to prey upon defenseless women. He was a lot like Charlie that way, and a lot like a certain Weasel whom Bolan knew.

Tom DeLuccia began his Mafia career as a leg-breaker for Castiglione, sadistic *capo* of the lower eastern seaboard. Arnie Farmer recognized a boy with talent, and DeLuccia was able to impress his boss with his dependability and flair for solving knotty problems. He was being groomed for a lieutenancy in Castiglione's bordello chain when trouble had materialized. Trouble's name was Bolan, and the rest was history.

The war had spanned an ocean, laying waste to family operations from Virginia to the British Isles. Arnie Farmer had personally tracked the blitzing bastard into London town, and he bought a different kind of farm entirely when Bolan made his stand. Back in the United States, DeLuccia was absorbed by Augie Marinello's creeping empire, spreading out of New York City and devouring adjacent territories. Bolan had returned in time to cripple Marinello in New York and finish him in Jersey, wiping out the Talifero boys along with their *padrone*, and Tommy was alone again, abandoned in the smoking rubble.

But DeLuccia was a natural survivor, and a good deal brighter than his mediocre ranking in the syndicate would indicate. Building from the ashes, he filled a power vacuum on the coast, expanding from his fiefdom in New Jersey, seizing opportunities that surfaced in the wake of Bolan's blitz. His specialties had always been narcotics, prostitution, smuggling; even in the old days, he was known as a man with overseas connections. He had been using those connections lately to entrench himself at the domestic end of a complex pipeline moving contraband— and slaves—around the globe.

The slavery angle had surprised Brognola, but when Bolan fed it to the Stony Man computers, circumstantial confirmation was available. DeLuccia's name had surfaced in connection with Battaglia's Heartland Produce, and his private number showed a history of regular communication with the Kansas *capo*. They were definitely connected, and the indicators pointed to DeLuccia as Benny's middleman, the East Coast connection. He would be the one to put it all together for Battaglia, cementing links with money men across the water. The Weasel's tracks were everywhere.

The working address for DeLuccia was a Newark warehouse on the dingy waterfront. Ostensibly, the owner was a Belco Shipping Company, but Tommy Weasel held the deed and pulled the strings. He moved a lot of merchandise from Newark—shipments out and goods received for distribution through the South and Midwest. Bolan had it on the best authority that one of Tommy's main import commodities was Turkish heroin refined and processed in the south of France.

As for the exports. . . .

Bolan would be checking into those himself.

DARKNESS COVERED NEWARK, and a thread of mist unraveled along the serpentine Passaic River. In the endless blackness, a foghorn sounded, quickly answered by a second and a third. The river was alive with giant gliding shapes, their voices haunting in the night.

Bolan wore the darkness like a cloak as he approached the Belco warehouse. Neighboring establishments were all deserted, but the soldier's target clung to signs of life. A light shone through frosted windowpanes; a Continental crew wagon was parked against the loading dock. DeLuccia was working late.

Bolan found a door beside the loading bay. He tried the lock and released it with a moment's effort. Easing his silenced pistol out of sideleather, double-checking the load, he slipped inside the warehouse proper. Deeper darkness enveloped him. Accustomed to conducting war in zero-visibility conditions, he progressed by feel along a narrow corridor, the muzzle of his 93-R probing ahead of him, ready to respond to any challenge. By the time he reached an elbow turn and started climbing wooden stairs, a light was faintly visible above him, shining underneath a door.

Bolan took the stairs with caution, testing each before he put his full weight down, alert to any sound that would betray his presence. Tommy Weasel had not posted any sentries, but the shadow warrior took no chances. He was halfway up the stairs when he heard a noise.

On the landing up above, the door abruptly opened on the darkness, framing a hulking figure in the sudden glare. Shuffling toward the stairs, the guy took a second to recognize the danger. When he spotted Bolan, frozen in the shaft of light, the gunner reacted and made the move that sealed his fate.

Despite his bulk, the hood had reacted smoothly and professionally. In other circumstances, against another adversary, his response would probably have been enough.

Bolan never let the gunman reach the holstered hardware he was groping for. His automatic stuttered, sending a trio of deadly parabellum manglers sizzling in on target, just above the gunner's nose. A scarlet halo wreathed the dead man's skull, and parts of him were outward bound before his mind could register death. Another second, and the nearly headless body vaulted backward through the doorway.

Bolan was following him all the way, bounding up the final flight of steps to salvage something from his small surprise advantage. He was standing in the open door as the mutilated corpse touched down. Bolan's eyes and weapon swept right around a cluttered office, taking hasty inventory.

There were three men grouped around a massive desk, regarding his arrival and their friend's departure with expressions of amazement. Bolan picked out his quarry at once—the close-set eyes and narrow, almost pointed face removed any doubts about the source of Tommy Weasel's nickname. Both the flankers carried side arms. They made a move to reach them as they broke the momentary spell of shock at his explosive entry.

Peeling off in opposite directions, clawing at the weapons underneath their jackets, the flankers were almost fast enough to get to Bolan.

Almost.

The qualifier was a fatal one, and it made all the difference in the world.

The gunner on his left was closer, marginally faster, so Bolan took him first. He left the pistol set for automatic fire and swiveled into target acquisition in a single fluid motion, stroking off a burst. At a range of twenty feet, it was impossible to miss his mark.

The Weasel's soldier seemed to stumble, reeling like a drunkard as the stunning triple punch came ripping in at chest level. The stumble turned into a sprawl, and Bolan watched him plow face first into hard, unyielding cabinets, rebounding awkwardly and landing in a crumpled, lifeless heap.

The second gunner was now claiming his attention, a rolling, diving figure on his right. The bastard's hand was on the pistol, just about to rip it free of leather, when the Bolan autoloader swept around to find him. Holes were stitched across his forehead. His skull exploded from the eyebrows up. Momentum carried him across the field of fire, but all the life and fight had left him now. The hood was a piece of meat in aimless, mindless motion, skimming on a slick of blood.

The Weasel stood alone before Mack Bolan, rooted in his place behind the desk. His rodent eyes were twitching back and forth between the bodies of his henchmen and their killer's face, the black Beretta leveled at his chest. The mouth was working, but it took him several tries to get it out.

"There's gotta be a way around this thing," he said, sounding hopeful rather than convinced.

"You're looking at it, Tommy."

Bolan let the muzzle of the automatic waggle, taking in the bodies at his feet.

DeLuccia was looking at it, and the little hoodlum was not liking what he saw. Behind the eyes, his agile mind was busy scanning options. "I'd like to make a deal," he offered, with a semblance of control.

"That's what I had in mind."

A flicker of encouragement showed in Tommy Weasel's twisted smile. "Yeah? All right. Just tell me what you want."

"The works," his captor told him. "All of it. The overseas connection you arranged for Ben Battaglia."

The cautious optimism faded, reappeared as something else. A deep, abiding fear, approaching panic. "Jesus, man. . . you ask a lot."

"You've got a lot to lose," the Executioner reminded him.

"Okay, but let me think a second, willya?"

Bolan lifted the Beretta, held her steady when the sights were leveled on DeLuccia's face. "Make it five," he told the Weasel. "One. . . ."

DeLuccia paled and began to tremble visibly, but there was still fight in him. "Some people got long arms, ya know?"

"With them, you've got a fighting chance. With me, it's over. Two...."

The Weasel stiffened, thrust out his chin defiantly. "You hafta unnerstand, I never ratted on a partner in my life." Extremity could not disguise a hint of pride.

"The ship's going down, Tommy. You can save yourself, or take the ride. Three...."

"You're handing me a death warrant," Tommy Weasel snapped, his voice becoming brittle.

"Four...."

"*All right.*" His hands were coming up, as if his open palms could fend off death. "Just take it easy." It took another moment for the guy to find his voice again. "I'm not in this as deep as you may think," he said. "A middleman, that's all."

The Executioner released a weary sigh and brought the automatic back on target. "Five."

A strangled scream escaped from Tommy Weasel's lips. The mobster looked as if he was about to faint. "A name," he shouted. "Jesus Christ, I swear it's all I know."

"I'm listening," the warrior told him softly.

DeLuccia took a ragged breath, held it briefly, then finally let it go. "The African connection, in Algiers," he said. "Guy calls himself Rani al-Haj."

Algiers. A tremor of the soul, and blackout curtains fell in place behind the graveyard eyes.

"He's the buyer?"

Tommy Weasel shrugged. "Buyer, seller... what the hell. It goes both ways."

"He takes the women off your hands." It was not a question. The soldier's voice was icing over, going cold and sharp as a scalpel blade.

"That's part of it. Battaglia bags the broads, and Rani comes across with this and that. Okay? I swear that's all I've got."

The Executioner had heard enough. He swallowed the revulsion, gave the little thug a look of withering contempt. "You stink of death," he said.

The Weasel blinked, his shiny little eyes constricting into pinpoints. "We had a deal," he croaked.

Bolan's answer was silence.

DeLuccia gave out a shriek of mingled fear and rage. He doubled over, grappling with a drawer and sobbing as it stubbornly resisted him. The gun was inside. Finally the drawer came free in his fevered grasp, and he grabbed for the piece.

Bolan held the trigger down and let his pistol empty out in autofire. Half a dozen parabellums picked the Weasel up and slammed him back against the plaster wall, descending slowly, by the inch. His passage left a vicious crimson smear on the fading paint.

"A deal's a deal, and you blew it," muttered Bolan as he fed another clip into his automatic.

He stowed the weapon back inside its armpit sheath and took himself away from there. The stench of blood and death was clinging to him when he reached the stairs; it made him anxious for the cool night air outside.

Bolan knew that he had barely scratched the surface, hardly made a dent in what was shaping up to be a major operation. In the next battle he would be revisiting Algiers.

The warrior closed his mind to memories and concentrated on the problem of the moment. Smiley—he would have to let her know that they had only just begun to fight.

The soldier found an exit and let himself out of the Belco warehouse. Gratefully, he let the silent darkness swallow him and carry him away.

5

Algiers.

The very name could be intimidating and enticing, full of secret terrors and the promise of forbidden pleasure. There is beauty in the land of Algeria, a solemn strength about its people—but beneath it all, a dark, compelling undercurrent of malignant evil, ancient as the soil.

Bolan knew the city, and the nation that had taken on its name. Together, they evoked a rush of bloody memories for him, akin to waking nightmares. From the early days of his crusade against the Mafia, Algiers had lured Bolan, haunted him, forever nagging at him from the cluttered corners of his mind. It was an open wound, a problem unresolved.

Early in his private war, crusader Bolan had encountered rumbles from Algeria. The battlefield had been France, and Bolan—*l'Américain formidable*—was engaged in mortal combat with the Mafia ambassador, Thomas "Monzoor" Rudolfi. Because the ladies of a syndicate *maison de joie* had assisted Bolan by giving him shelter, they were slated for a ghastly punishment, designed to serve Rudolfi as a warning and an example to their sisters of the street. Ten of them had been scheduled to be sold at an auction—human chattel in the secret, teeming markets of Algiers.

Desperate action was imperative, and Bolan had reacted with a grim audacity to thwart Rudolfi's plan. The Executioner's scheme had been simple—a ranking member of the syndicate would die for every hour that the ladies were in jeopardy. And die they did. Eventually, Rudolfi had capitulated under fire...and he lost it all when the flames devoured his Parisian fiefdom.

It was another time, another war, when Bolan—as Colonel John Phoenix—had paid his initial visit to Algiers. The enemy was terrorism, and his mission was vital: the daughter of a U.S. high-tech engineer was missing, ransomed for the secret of a low-yield nuclear device her father had developed. Bolan found a trail, pursued it doggedly and ended up alone against a mercenary army in the Tanezrouft—a grim Saharan no-man's-land 800 miles south of Algiers. In what had started as a mercy mission, he encountered evidence of terrorism orchestrated on a global scale.

And it was not a new idea, by any means. The Mafia had coined a term for it—*cosa di tutti cosi*: literally the "Big Thing"—and tried many times to give it life before the blitzing bastard out of Pittsfield, Mass., brought their house down.

Luke Harker, aging U.S. radical with messianic tendencies, had been in the driver's seat when Bolan hit Algiers. Harker's master plan—creation of a super camp for training terrorists of every stripe—was nearing ultimate fruition when the Phoenix fighter intervened. Harker called his troop the Third World People's Liberation Front, but there were other hands upon the helm. The Soviets were interested, and their man in Harker's camp was the notorious Riccardo Roybal, better known to Interpol as Rikki the Hyena. Bolan took them on en masse and blazed a trail of death across the desert sands before he brought the enemy to heel. Scorched earth in the Sahara, a cleansing flame to sear away the evidence of Harker's evil.

But the evil lingered on in Algiers, and Bolan had returned. This time, the cancer was an ancient one, with deep tenacious roots imbedded in the rocky desert soil.

It was the blight of slavery, and its origins were traceable across the centuries.

6

The dancer made another pirouette, putting her body into it, with feeling. Her skimpy harem outfit—the snug, embroidered top and bottoms of diaphanous material, with nothing underneath—accented her fine figure. She had olive skin, flashing eyes, and black hair that fell almost to her waist.

She moved with a fluid grace that was hypnotic, keeping time to music only she could hear. Her breasts responded to the writhing of her body, and they bounced and shimmered in the dusky light. Her skin, glistening with sweat, seemed to melt as she abandoned herself to the sinuous pulse of her dance. She vibrated with rapture, careless of the effect—beyond any caring or hope. She was wet from the exertion, dazed by the music and the sensations of her own throbbing body, so that all the reality around her seemed like a mist. She was lost in a Garden of Earthly Delights, imprisoned in an eternity of adolescent turmoil, sucked too deep into the turbulence of a will abandoned to the belly, to willpower entranced by a feeling in the groin.

Lounging in his thronelike wicker chair, Rani al-Haj watched the woman spin and undulate in front of him, narrow eyes devouring every inch of her. He felt a tightness in his groin and shifted uncomfortably, crossing his meaty legs. The wicker groaned underneath his weight.

The girl would work out nicely, he decided. The patrons of his club were constantly in search of something new, exciting. This one was a skillful dancer, and she might have other talents. If she proved amenable, perhaps he could direct her into other avenues of commerce on the side...and make a profit for himself, of course.

Rani was accustomed to regarding people with disdain, as objects, bits of merchandise. It was an attitude he had cultivated during his thirty-seven years, developing a taste for power and the privileges that went with it. There were times, even recently, when he had been consumed with thoughts of day-to-day survival; but his instinct and cunning always confirmed that a patient man can watch and wait, seize the opportunities presented to him. And Rani was a living monument to perseverance.

In his blood there flowed the very history of occupied Algeria. His father was a wealthy French *colon*, his mother an attractive Arab native. The fruit of their clandestine coupling was squat and dark, an animated social blemish and perpetual reminder of the gap between the ruling classes and their subjects. Rani's father had predictably ignored his obligation, spurned the woman who embarrassed him, and his mother, after failing as a beggar, joined the ranks of Casbah prostitutes in order to keep them both alive.

One night, when Rani was fifteen, she quarreled with a drunken Legionnaire about her price; she tried to stab the man when he refused to pay, but he was stronger, faster. Rani had come home to find his mother dead in a pool of blood, the single dinar clutched tenaciously in one small hand. He swore an oath of vengeance on the French, the wealthy—anyone who stood between himself and power.

There were gales of revolution rising in Algiers, and orphan Rani let them carry him away, the cause and its requirements devouring a portion of his pain, his loneliness. He became acquainted with the National Liberation Front and helped plot their raids against the hated Legionnaires. A scion of the streets, he made himself at home wherever foreign troops and officers were found, selecting targets for the bombers who would follow after. Once, the Arab tried his hand at demolition, but the satchel of plastique he place inside a hotel lobby failed to detonate, and Rani watched in grim humiliation as his enemies continued with their lives, unscathed.

A week before the final independence, Rani stole a pistol, hiked the forty miles from Algiers to his father's grand estate, and crept inside. He intended to slay the man who had shamed his mother and abandoned him at birth, but he found the place deserted, picked clean as part of the ongoing French evacuation. It was the story of his life—too little and too late. . . at least until recently.

Three years earlier, a chain of burglaries and drug transactions had provided him with enough working capital to buy the ancient Club Grandee and put himself in business. Now he dealt in liquor, dabbled in the sale of hashish with some small-time prostitution on the side. But his final hope for wealth—his one last chance to become a member of the ruling class that he was taught to hate from childhood—lay with his involvement in a larger, grander scheme.

He was close and could almost taste the fruits of final victory. And the anticipation of success affected Rani like a potent aphrodisiac. He longed to seize the power, to possess it totally.

In front of him, the dancer writhed and twisted. Rani stared at her, transfixed. She almost seemed to have forgotten him, surrendered to the rhythm of her dance. He rose impatiently out of the wicker throne and clapped his hands together, instantly commanding her attention.

At a word, she came to him, unquestioning. She stood in front of Rani, silent, with her eyes downcast as pudgy fingers found the fasteners of her top. Rani slipped the fasteners open, freed her breasts. He reached out to cup them in his palms, but was distracted by a rapping on the outer door.

"Come," Rani said as the woman covered herself.

The door was opened and Rani's Tuareg bodyguard, Amal, appeared. Amal swept the private office with a glance, identified the woman and dismissed her as insignificant, the flat, black eyes returning automatically to Rani. Amal had little use for women at the best of times; now, his posture and the furrow of his brow bespoke preoccupation.

"A visitor," the Tuareg said. "American."

His voice was taut, and the act of speaking sent an ugly ripple through the razor scar along his cheek.

Rani frowned and shook his head. He was expecting no one. "Not today," he answered. "Take a message. Have him call for an appointment."

Amal was suddenly uneasy, his discomfort obvious. To Rani, the knife-fighter's air of hesitancy meant trouble. "He says DeLuccia is dead."

The stocky Arab tried to mask his shock, but he could never fool Amal. The two of them had been together much too long. "I'll see him. Let me have a moment first."

When the Tuareg had removed himself, Rani turned to the woman. "Business takes priority, my dove." He deftly slipped a key into her hand. "My private chamber is above. Wait for me there."

The dancer bowed, kissed his hand, then retreated toward the exit and the stairs beyond. When she was gone, he leaned across his desk and keyed a button on the intercom. Another moment and Amal was ushering the unexpected visitor inside.

Rani took a second to assess the man before he spoke. The stranger was a full head shorter than Amal but muscular, athletic-looking, broad across the chest and shoulders. An air of quiet menace radiated from the man, and Rani did not overlook the bulge a pistol made beneath the tastefully expensive jacket of his suit.

And the Arab recognized a killer when he saw one. "Welcome to Club Grandee, effendi. I am the proprietor."

"LaMancha, Frank," the stranger introduced himself. "We need to talk some business."

"Ah."

LaMancha glanced at Rani's bouncer from the corner of his eye and waited. Rani nodded to Amal, and the lanky Tuareg left them, closing the door. The stocky nightclub owner settled into a padded chair behind his desk.

"The business?"

The newcomer made himself at home, perching on a corner of the desk, lighting a cigarette before he answered. "Tommy Weasel's dead. You need a new connection."

Rani spread his hands and made a show of ignorance. "I'm afraid—"

"You should be," LaMancha interrupted. "There's enough heat to go around."

The Arab felt his anger and confusion mounting, but did his best to cover both. "You speak in riddles. How am I to understand?"

"I'll make it simple for you, Rani. There's a war on. You need to pick a side."

"Assuming that you speak the truth, how does it relate to me?"

"A salesman needs suppliers. You're fresh out."

"DeLuccia...."

"Had an accident," the stranger finished. "Write him off."

Rani smiled without humor. "He has—how do you say it—connections of his own."

"Had," the tall American corrected. "Make it past tense. They're out of it."

"I see." In truth, he did not understand at all. Rani needed time to think, but this American, LaMancha, seemed to want his answers in a hurry. He was pushing, forcing Rani back into a corner.

As if in answer to the Arab's thoughts, La-Mancha leaned across the broad expanse of desk, his jacket falling open to reveal the holstered pistol.

"I don't have a lot of time," he growled, "and you don't either. Look around you, man. It's time to shit or get off the pot."

Rani grimaced at LaMancha's turn of phrase. Despite his hedonistic life-style, he found profanity offensive. Worse, the visitor's insistence made it difficult for him to organize his thoughts.

"I am not in a position to negotiate with you."

"Oh?" LaMancha's voice had frosted over, blue gray eyes turning flinty, cold.

"I have superiors to deal with. They must be informed, consulted."

"Well, dammit."

"Surely you must understand. The business—"

"Could blow away before you finish playing with yourself." LaMancha slammed an open palm against the desk top, making pens and pencils dance. "You're telling me there's nothing you can do?"

"Until I speak with my superiors—"

"Yeah, yeah, all right." LaMancha waved the explanation off. "Get on the horn and pull some strings. You could lose it by tomorrow, things are happening so fast."

Rani nodded, feeling perspiration on his upper lip. "I understand."

"You'd better." LaMancha's tone was menacing as he slid off the desk and started circling the office. "Screw this up, and there won't be a hole you can hide in."

Anger jostled with the awe his visitor inspired, and Rani felt the color rising in his cheeks. With an effort, he controlled his temper. "I will pass your message on. If there is any word—"

"Twelve hours," Frank LaMancha snapped. "I'll give you that. If your people can't get on the stick, I'll have to find another buyer."

Rani stiffened. This American was more than crude and domineering; he was crazy. It was not advisable to argue with a lunatic, especially when he wore a pistol underneath his arm.

"I understand your urgency. If there is someplace I can reach you in Algiers."

"I'm at the Orient. You know it?"

Rani nodded, picturing the old hotel on rue de la Révolution. It did not fit LaMancha's image. "Yes," he answered. "I will be in touch."

LaMancha pinned him with an icy glare.

"Twelve hours, Rani. That's all I've got. It's all *you've* got."

Rani felt the ice begin to crystallize around his spine. "A threat?"

LaMancha hesitated at the door and turned to face him. "A promise. Twelve hours max." He aimed a finger at the desk-top telephone. "You've got a call to make."

The heavy door clicked shut behind LaMancha, and the Arab found himself alone. For an instant he could feel the office shrinking, closing in around him. The air was heavy, threatening to smother him.

He would have to make the call, of course. Whatever LaMancha proved to be, Rani did not have the option of ignoring him. His people had to be informed without delay.

His people.

Rani's frown became a brooding scowl. It was the other way around, in actuality; *he* belonged to *them*. A temporary situation, if the Arab had his way, but for the moment very real.

He hesitated with a hand upon the telephone. One call would do the job, and Rani knew that timing was essential. His function was to act as go-between, an agent; he was not expected to provide solutions. That was left to others, and the Arab did not envy their responsibility.

He could alert the countess, but on second thought . . . .

Rani knew it had to be the Corsican, Armand. He was the strategist, the brains. Armand would have an answer for LaMancha when he heard the news.

The Arab sat immobile for a moment with the telephone receiver in his hand, dial tone humming like a distant air-raid siren. Ancient sultans had made a practice of eliminating messengers when news was bad, and Rani's message had to be the worst Armand would hear today. DeLuccia's death, the rumor of a war disrupting trade with the United States. . . .

A sour taste invaded Rani's mouth, his stomach shifted, rolling like a raft at sea. He felt as if the floor beneath his feet might split open at any moment, dropping him into a black abyss. The woman waiting for him in the upstairs chamber was forgotten as he concentrated on the problem of survival.

Salvaging the wreck was Armand's job. Rani, at the moment, was concerned with salvaging himself.

At last, reluctantly, he bowed to the inevitable and started dialing.

7

Dusty noonday heat assaulted Bolan as he put the Club Grandee behind him. Turning left, keeping an eye open for a tail, he moved with loping strides along a narrow, bustling street. Sidewalk vendors and pedestrians regarded him with casual curiosity, but something in his manner kept them at bay. The beggars, prostitutes and pickpockets let him pass undisturbed; the barkers knew at once that he was not a customer. And Bolan—alias LaMancha—gave them no more than a passing thought as he brushed through their ranks, intent upon his mission.

He was concentrating on Rani and the information he had gathered from their interview. The meeting had progressed according to his plan, with satisfactory results. He had not expected Rani to begin negotiations on his own; the point of his appearance at the Club Grandee had been to rattle the proprietor and send him running to his hidden masters for advice. It was a tried and tested part of Bolan's three-phase battle plan.

Infiltration.

Identification.

Execution.

Urgency never equated with carelessness in Bolan's world. An uninformed warrior not only jeopardized himself, he ran a risk of striking down the innocent, allowing enemies to slip away. When the Phoenix fighter closed in on this particular vipers' nest, all the serpents would be safely bundled up inside. And all would die. A clean sweep.

Rani would be running scared, for sure. Bolan recognized the signs and knew the stocky Arab did not have the guts or the initiative to handle this one by himself. He would try to pass the heat along, unload the burden, and Bolan meant to join him for the hand-off.

A long block down from the Grandee, he found the rented Audi in its place beside the curb. A slender youth was perched on the fender like a giant hood ornament, narrow eyes devouring the street around him. At the Executioner's approach, he scrambled down and took up station by the car, his face and attitude expectant.

Bolan gave the car a rapid inspection, discovering nothing out of place. His lookout palmed the promised dinars, flashed a crooked grin and sauntered off along the sloping street. Bolan knew the boy would sell his license number and description to the highest bidder, but he was not concerned. The Audi had been rented under his LaMancha pseudonym, his address listed as the Orient . . . all a part of the facade.

He settled in behind the wheel, removing a miniature receiver from an inside jacket pocket. He placed the tiny earplug into place, and turned up the volume control, frowning as silence emanated from the instrument.

Bolan's visit to Rani's nightclub had been tactically as well as psychologically inspired. The Executioner had fastened a tiny limpet microphone underneath the lip of Rani's massive desk. In ideal conditions, the device possessed a one-mile working radius, but here—allowing for the labyrinthine streets and buildings crowded in—line-of-sight was necessary.

Besides, Bolan wanted visual contact when the Arab made his move.

He was picking up some restless, shifting sounds from the office, then he heard Rani dialing the telephone. Bolan waited through another momentary silence, then the Arab started speaking rapidly, excitedly. The bug would only give him Rani's side of the conversation, but with any luck at all, it might just be enough.

Bolan listened, cursing to himself as Rani babbled on—in French. It had been a long shot. In old Algiers, the language of colonialism lingered on, and English-speaking residents were a large minority, at best. The Executioner had bet against the odds, and he had come up short.

He was not bilingual, though a double tour in Vietnam—another erstwhile French possession—taught him fragments of the language. He could make out snatches of the Arab's monologue, a sentence here and there amid the verbal rapid-fire.

Rani was arguing with someone named Armand. The names LaMancha and DeLuccia kept surfacing, and frequently the Arab had to stop, repeating something for his listener. Armand was trying to make sense of Rani's verbal avalanche, apparently demanding repetition for the sake of clarity. Toward the end of the conversation, Rani's tone was more subdued; he was agreeing with whatever his connection had to say. *"Oui,"* the small, metallic voice was saying, *"Oui*, Armand."

The telephone receiver rattled in its cradle, and the Arab slammed a fist against his desk, cursing to himself. *"Merde."*

Bolan grinned. He could translate that one for himself.

The little Arab was unhappy with his orders, but the Executioner was certain he would follow them. The tone he used when speaking to Armand betrayed the fear that Rani felt for his superiors. For *this* superior, at any rate.

Rani would comply with his instructions, and

if Bolan could stay with him, there was a good chance he would find the author of those orders waiting at the other end of the line.

One more rung on the ladder.

And phase one of Bolan's strategy, infiltration, had already been accomplished. Bolan had a foothold in Algiers.

The second phase, identification of the enemy, was in the works. Rani was his key to picking out the players, lining up his targets for the strike.

Finally, when that had been achieved, he would be ready for the third and final phase.

Execution.

It was the reason for his presence in Algiers, the bottom line in Bolan's fight against terrorism.

There was no compromise with evil, with the cannibals. A savvy warrior answered terrorism in the universal language. Fire against fire. Gun against gun.

And the Executioner was fluent in *that* language. No interpreters were needed, no translation necessary. It was all a matter of determining who got the final word.

He was ready, waiting, when the Citroën sedan emerged from the alley next to Rani's Club Grandee. He glimpsed the Arab's profile in the back seat, caught the look of consternation on his face before the chauffeur turned the car away from him and merged with other traffic.

Bolan gave his prey the lead, counting to ten before he put the Audi into motion. Cars were not uncommon in the Casbah, but even so, discretion was the better part of valor. He could ill afford to spook the Arab, lose him in the twisting maze of streets and watch his only lead evaporate. His hopes were riding in the Citroën, and if he lost it now. . . .

Bolan put the germ of doubt and grim defeatism out of his mind. He would stick with Rani, keep the Citroën in sight because he had to. For the mission, for Smiley and for himself.

Smiley Dublin was sequestered in a local safehouse, procured by Stony Man Farm. She was protected, but chafing at the bit and aching for an active role. Bolan knew the feeling and understood her restlessness, but there were still foundations to be laid. He was not committing Smiley—or himself—to anything before a working strategy was formulated.

It was time for groundwork now. Smiley would have to live with her impatience for a while.

Bolan was on the hunt.

8

Algiers is a city with many faces: seat of government and teeming slum; commercial center and focus of a nation's intellectual life. Here the rich and powerful exist in close proximity to hopeless thousands; they occupy the city's space together, but they do not touch.

The heart of old Algiers is in the Casbah, an ancient labyrinth of narrow, twisting streets. It is a shopper's paradise...and haven for the city's underworld, a haven for scum. From the old fortress, drivers and pedestrians may zigzag downward past the old patriarchal houses, homing on the Cemetery of the Princesses, the Mosque of Sidi-Abderahmane and the Grand Mosque. Detached from the maze are the more serene and up-to-date surroundings of the Admiralty. From here, the Barbary pirates launched their raids in bygone days, a distant memory now. To eastward lies a fishing port, the markets at the Pecherie and, higher up, commanding all the city from its regal overlook is the Mustafa Superieur, complete with former summer palace of the gov-

ernor and two museums. Beyond the city proper, the Bay of Algiers is lined with scenic
beaches, fishing villages and stylish resorts that
feature fine hotels and water sports, luxury
cafes and grand casinos. At the far end of the
bay is Sidi Fredj, a spacious holiday resort.

Rani al-Haj had spent a lifetime in Algiers
without attaining any power or respect. The
stocky Arab meant to change all that, and soon.
He had an angle now, a new approach and new
associates who offered something better. He
had learned from them, was learning still, devouring the lessons they discarded casually, un-
thinkingly. He would dominate them all, in
time. Provided he could anticipate the dangers,
deal with unexpected problems swiftly and deci-
sively. Provided he did not fumble now, with
every eye upon him.

If he lost it now, the dream would turn to
ashes. If LaMancha spoke the truth about a
looming war, it would require tenacity, intelligence and courage to survive.

Rani hoped that he was equal to the challenge.

The Citroën bore him up and into el-Biar, a
fashionable suburb west of old Algiers, halfway
up the sloping Sahel hills. Below, if he had cared
to look, the high-rise buildings of the capital
were plainly visible, but Rani's eyes were blind
to his immediate surroundings. He would have

to have some answers ready for Armand, but at the moment Rani was not even certain of the questions.

Slowing, the driver brought him to the gateway of an elegant estate. Inside the fence, a uniformed attendant with a pistol on his hip was with them instantly, checking the car and occupants before keying the gate's locking mechanism. The Citroën passed through, proceeding along the curving drive.

The house was huge, palatial. Once a private hideaway for foreign diplomats before the revolution, it had passed to other hands of late, but it was still a seat of power—hidden now, covert.

Rani saw the others had arrived ahead of him. He recognized the countess's sleek Mercedes parked behind Mustaffa's cream-colored Rolls. He experienced a sinking feeling in his stomach as his driver found a spot beside the Mercedes and killed the engine.

They would all be waiting for him, hungry eyes and stabbing questions, all demanding information, reassurance that the status quo could be preserved. Another moment and he would be in the dock, a witness at the inquisition.

He left the Citroën, walked up the marble steps, and by the time he reached the double oak doors, a butler was holding them open for him.

He was ushered through an entryway connected to a casual dining room the size of a tennis court. The northern wall was made of glass, with sliding doors that opened on a broad veranda.

The vultures were arranged around an oblong table, waiting for him as he joined them on the patio. Silk-suited flankers, obviously armed, were stationed all around the terrace, scanning the terrain below the house. Rani wondered whether they were there to keep him in or to keep intruders out. No one brought a chair for the Arab, and he stood before the table examining the trio who controlled his fate.

On his left, the countess, Ilse Brunow, watched him with a trace of dark amusement in her eyes. She was enjoying his predicament, and Rani knew that she would be no help to him, whatever happened. They had been associates for longer than he cared to remember, and Rani owed much of his present status to her backing. But she would sacrifice him willingly with pleasure if it came to that.

To his right, the Saudi, Mustaffa Assad, was watching Rani through the mirrored lenses of his aviator's glasses. If Assad was feeling anything at all, he hid it well, his face as impassive as a slab of beef.

In front of Rani, like a buffer placed between Mustaffa and the countess, sat Armand Dusault. Urbane, sophisticated, he would be the one to watch. The bare suggestion of a scowl that played across his face was frightening, indicative of anger that could reach a lethal flash point without warning. This man was Death, and when he spoke, his voice was like the rustle of a midnight breeze across an unkempt grave.

"So, Rani."

And he waited, letting Rani stand in front of him, perspiring in the sun. In another moment, when the Arab lingered on in awkward silence, he continued.

"I have confirmation from our colleagues in America. Both DeLuccia and Battaglia are out of business. Permanently."

Rani swallowed hard. "I understand."

"You do? Perhaps you could explain it to the rest of us."

The Arab stiffened, recognizing the trap too late. "As I told you, this LaMancha spoke of trouble in America. A war?"

"Of course," Armand replied. "And who are the combatants, Rani? The Mafia, perhaps? De-Luccia and Battaglia *were* the Mafia."

"The families fight among themselves, Armand."

"Naturally," Armand said with a mocking smile. "But I have spoken with a member of the ruling council, *La Commissióne*, and he assures me that our late associates were well-respected men of honor. *Non*, Rani, this is not a war of brothers.''

Rani could think of no reply, but the countess spared him momentarily. "Perhaps the competition," she suggested.

Armand raised an eyebrow, half turned to face her. "Please elaborate."

Her shrug was graceful, almost sensual.

"The United States is an ethnic mosaic, darling. Blacks and Latins, Haitians and Orientals—all hungry for the good life they see on television. They have infiltrated every walk of life, Armand. Your *mafiosi* can't control them anymore."

Dusault was nodding thoughtfully. "There is truth in what you say, but my contacts in America would surely be aware of any such assault by outside forces. They have no motive for deceiving us."

"The motive may not be apparent," she replied.

Mustaffa cleared his throat, a rumbling interjection that demanded their attention. "There is another possibility," he said. "We must not overlook political considerations."

Both the countess and Armand appeared confused. The sheikh explained himself. "There are radicals—guerrillas—in America and elsewhere, who crave attention, notoriety. Some of them would gladly risk their lives for—what do you say—a piece of the action.''

"Possibly," Armand said. But he was not convinced.

Mustaffa frowned and folded hands across his ample stomach. "Then again, there is the government itself," he added.

Armand's frown was carving furrows in his face. "Explain."

The Saudi sipped his ice water, taking his time. "Every government has agencies designed to handle special situations. Propaganda and intelligence, assassination. . . ."

Armand released a weary sigh and shook his head. "Improbable," he answered. "Americans assassinate reformers and their favorite presidents. The criminal enjoys a high degree of constitutional protection; he is pampered, often elevated to the status of a folk hero."

"Who, then?" Mustaffa asked.

"Who, indeed." The Corsican was facing Rani, full attention again focused on the little Arab. "This LaMancha may be able to enlighten us. You will arrange the meeting he desires—tonight, at Club Grandee. If he cannot explain himself. . . ."

Armand did not complete the sentence, but he left no doubt about his meaning or intentions. Frank LaMancha *would* explain himself, or he would never leave Algiers alive.

Dusault was watching Rani, gray eyes boring into him, laying bare his soul. Rani felt as if he was an item on the luncheon menu. Cannibals were gathering for the feast, and suddenly he needed to be out of there, to put some ground between himself and his superiors.

"A drink before you go?" The tone and Armand's expression told Rani not to accept the offer.

"No," he answered. "Thank you, but I have to make some calls."

"Of course. Phillipe will see you out."

At a gesture from Dusault, the nearest guard started toward them, lumbering across the patio. Rani was observing him peripherally, alert but unprepared for what happened.

Phillipe was ten feet away when he appeared to stumble, losing his balance. Simultaneously, the gunner's skull exploded like a melon with a firecracker inside, flesh and bone and brains erupting in a liquid halo. The headless body seem to float with arms outstretched, a ghastly human butterfly, impacting in the center of Armand's veranda table.

Glasses toppled, smashing on the flagstones, liquor mingling with the oily slick of blood. A spray of blood caught the countess, dark droplets soaking through her silken caftan. Mustaffa and Armand were scrambling from their seats.

Rani was still gaping at the body when a second gunner on his right was shot down. The soldier tried to shout, but the only sound that issued from his throat was that of wind and liquid rushing through a ragged hole the size of Rani's fist. The light of life had flickered out behind the hardman's eyes before his legs began to buckle. He flopped backward like a leaking bag of grain.

And Rani heard the gunfire. The first reports were rolling in on top of one another like a distant thunder. Survivors of the palace guard were pulling back to cover their employer and his guests, remove them from the line of fire. Rani broke his momentary trance; he was racing for the house and sanctuary when the next rounds started sizzling in.

A pair of soldiers had Armand between them, hustling him across the patio when death overtook them. On the left, a flanker lost his stride and half his face, a frothy geyser splattering Dusault. The Corsican was still recoiling when he lost the other escort to a second thundering round. The dying trooper lurched across his path and Armand stumbled over him, collapsing on his hands and knees amid the human rubble.

Rani reached the sliding doors and threw himself headlong into the dining room. Scrambling along the floor in search of cover, he could not escape the grim kaleidoscope of violence just beyond the threshold. Armand was struggling to his feet, Mustaffa and the countess were clutching each other helplessly behind the meager shield provided by the upturned table. All around them, soldiers scrambled, dodged and died.

The Arab pressed his face against the floor, locking arms above his head to block the tolling thunder. Rani aged a dozen years in as many seconds, offering a string of desperate prayers. When the firing finally ended, it took another moment for his mind to register the silence.

Rough hands seized him by the collar, jerked him to his knees. A twisted, bloody face was glaring at him, inches from his own, and Rani scarcely recognized the dapper Corsican beneath his dripping war paint.

Dusault was shouting at him, shaking him. Rani had to concentrate on his words in order to make sense of them.

"This is your doing. You have brought this curse upon my house." Armand was trembling. "I want this LaMancha, do you hear me? *Do you understand?*"

The violent trembling became a part of Rani. He tried to answer, but his tongue refused to function. He nodded frantically, a spastic signal of assent.

He understood the Corsican, of course, and recognized the blood lust in his eyes. Armand had been insulted, challenged, and he would exact a chilling retribution. Rani could produce LaMancha. . . or he would die.

A natural survivor, Rani saw his options and made the only logical decision.

He would sacrifice the tall American.

He would survive.

9

Early in his military tour, Mack Bolan learned the benefits and nuances of mental warfare. He had trained himself to penetrate the hostile mind as well as enemy defenses, turning the mind against its owner as a lethal weapon. Frightened enemies were careless, sloppy; they made mistakes, and those mistakes were often fatal.

A soldier who could start out rattling his adversaries entered battle with a firm advantage, and the Phoenix warrior was an expert rattler.

He had done some rattling that very afternoon in el-Biar. A probing strike, designed to get the enemy's attention, let him have a taste of hell. It was an appetizer before the bloody entrée.

Rani was his stalking horse, a human key to open the slavers' circle. He had taken Bolan one step farther up the ladder, brought him into striking range. Bolan could have taken out his contacts, picked them off of the veranda with his Weatherby .460, but caution stayed his hand.

The Executioner was shooting for annihilation in Algiers, with all the players present and accounted for. He had to *know* no one had been overlooked.

And so he had studied Rani's contacts, scrutinizing them through the rifle's twenty-power scope. From half a mile away he watched them sipping drinks. He could have hit them then, but he opted for a calculated miss.

The soldiers were expendable, but in dying they would get his point across. Ranking slavers would react out of necessity, and thus expose themselves. The second phase of Bolan's strategy—identification—would be accomplished.

When the enemy responded to his probe, the Executioner intended to be ready, waiting. He was on the move before the echoes of his gunfire died away in el-Biar, preparing to absorb the counterthrust and turn it back on his adversaries.

They would be expecting Frank LaMancha, *mafioso*. What they would find would be a slice of hell.

Bolan knew time was of the essence as he entered his hotel on rue de la Révolution. The Orient had been a looker once, but times and fashions changed. Tired facilities and sluggish service sent the tourists off in search of other lodgings, and the hostelry was fading fast.

It was ideal for Bolan's purposes.

His "suite"—a single room with a dingy bath adjacent—was located on the second floor front. He had procured the room as a convenience, and he was prepared to depart. But first, some preparations had to be made.

The enemy would look for him here. Bolan prepared a special greeting for his opposition, dropping a lethal welcome mat at the threshold.

He removed every vestige of himself from the room. When the troops arrived to take him, they would find exactly what he wanted them to find, nothing more. A plastic charge was mounted on the door, and Bolan deftly set the radio-remote explosive cap in place. The charge was small, designed for flash and fury on a relatively minor scale—he had no intention of demolishing the place. It was an antipersonnel device, and it would serve his needs.

Directly opposite the door, he left a miniature transceiver standing on the coffee table, sensitive receptors angled toward the entrance of the room. Bolan was abandoning the place, but he would be informed and ready to react if anyone should force the door. In fact, he was counting on it.

Satisfied, the warrior took his leave. He locked the door behind him, left a Do Not Disturb sign posted to discourage the hotel's arthritic maid. Anyone who tried the door in

Bolan's absence would be hostile, and he was declaring open season on the savages.

He took the back way out of the hotel, content to walk around the block, evading the danger of surveillance on the street. It was unlikely that the slavers had a shadow on him yet, but Bolan never took unnecessary chances. Vigilance and caution were the keys to his survival in the killing grounds.

Night was falling over old Algiers, the creeping darkness huddling into alleyways and corners. Dusk would bring the predators to life, transform the inner city from a picturesque attraction to a jungle, where survival of the fittest was the rule. A predator himself, and long accustomed to the jungle darkness, Bolan felt at home there.

The night could be his friend, his shelter. Enemies who sought him in the darkness might discover more than they had bargained for.

A noose was closing in Algiers, a hangman's harness snugging tight around the savage throat. A grim, relentless Executioner was ready now to spring the trap.

And there was nothing left to do but wait.

RANI KNEW THE CITY AFTER DARK. He was a creature of the streets, familiar with their perils and rewards, at home among the denizens of darkness. Lately, though, the friendly night had undergone a change...and in place of his confidence, he now encountered fear.

A new and lethal presence was emerging in Algiers. He could not attach a name or face to it, but Rani recognized the danger. Worse, he had been put in charge of its elimination, ordered to repair the damage and prevent its spread throughout the city. If he failed....

Rani double-checked the action of his Walther automatic pistol. He withdrew the magazine, verified the load, replaced it and pumped the slide to chamber a 9mm round. The pistol's weight was reassuring in his fist.

Armand had ordered him to bring LaMancha in alive, and Rani meant to do his best. But there were other dangers in the dark, and he was prepared for all of them. He did not intend to die for the cartel.

If it came to killing, Rani would rely upon his crew—a score of thugs and cutthroats. He had used them all before, when there was need of muscle on the streets, and they were waiting for him now behind the tavern.

It was a hunting party, and the prey was Frank LaMancha. Rani recognized a case of overkill, but he was playing safe. The quarry would not slip away from him because he had arrived shorthanded. He would try to reason with LaMancha, but if the American would not listen, he would smother him.

Rani had his doubts that LaMancha was the sniper who had struck at el-Biar. It made no sense for him to offer warnings in advance if he was planning an offensive of his own. And as for motive. . . .

No, it seemed more likely that another enemy had followed the American to Rani and Armand. LaMancha was an opportunist, seeking profit from the troubles in America, but violence had pursued him to Algiers.

Rani had left Amal in charge of operations at the club. The Tuareg was his hole card, too valuable to risk, and Rani wanted him available in case of any trouble. He had enough troops to handle Frank LaMancha.

A private exit brought him to the alleyway. A line of cars awaited him, his Citroën at the point, and every gunner present was alert to his approach. Some of them were smoking; the smell of hashish was oppressive in the narrow alley.

Rani scowled, but kept his anger to himself. He would accomplish nothing by lecturing the troops. The damage had been done; there was no time for any change of plans or substitution in the ranks.

He would have to watch them closely now. Some of them were nervous, trigger-happy at the best of times, and they might kill LaMancha if they imagined any danger to themselves. Armand was adamant in his desire to question the American, and it was Rani's job to bring him back alive.

Rani took a seat beside the Citroën's driver, nodding to the gunners in the rear, and issued orders to go to the Orient. The little caravan started, vehicles running in tandem through the winding streets.

They reached the Orient and parked in front of the hotel. Rani huddled with his troops, selecting half a dozen to accompany him inside, detailing others to surround the aging structure. The guards outside would prevent LaMancha from escaping if he managed to evade the spearhead. No American would cross their line without a pass from Rani.

When all guns were in position, Rani led his main contingent through the double doors, across a musty lobby toward the stairs. A call placed earlier had given him LaMancha's room number, and now the Arab took his force directly to the target area.

Upstairs, the Orient looked older, more dilapidated than its public face. The carpet was discolored, bald in spots, and faded tapestries were hung strategically to mask stains on the walls. A smell of dust and dampness was pervasive, almost overpowering.

Rani led his team along the dingy corridor until they reached the door of Frank LaMancha's room. A light was visible beneath the door; suspended from the tarnished knob, a sign advised that the occupant was not to be disturbed.

Rani retreated to an alcove twenty paces down the corridor. He slipped a hand inside his jacket and withdrew the Walther, gesturing with it toward the door.

His men could take the point and bring La-Mancha out. If something happened, if it fell apart, Rani would be waiting in the plug position with his pistol primed and ready. Just in case.

And privately, he could acknowledge that it would be safer where he was, beyond the line of fire.

Always, Rani was a cautious man.

His soldiers had their weapons out, a ring of flesh and steel outside LaMancha's door. One gunner knocked, waited, received no answer and tried again without result. Rani, at his post, experienced a sudden chill, the fleeting premonition of disaster. When the ranking gunman looked to him for guidance, he swallowed hard and nodded.

Momentary hesitation as the ranks were closed, then a boot heel slammed against the door. The locking mechanism splintered, flew apart; the way was open, gunners crowded into the room and out of Rani's sight. Excited voices were suddenly devoured by a smoky thunderclap.

A ball of hungry flame erupted from the doorway of LaMancha's room, expelling human wreckage in a grisly rush. Deafened, Rani staggered under the force of the shock wave, certain that the old hotel was coming down around him. Plaster sifted down and mingled with the acrid smoke of battle, threatening to choke him.

Rani shouted to his soldiers, but there was no answer in the charnel house. His men were dead or dying, fodder for the spreading fire, and there was nothing he could do to help them.

But LaMancha....

Rani had to satisfy himself, prepare an answer for Armand. He left the shelter of his niche, proceeding down the corridor on trembling legs. The Walther probed ahead of him, alert to any challenge from the ruins.

He was halfway to the door when automatic weapons' fire erupted in the street below. Frantic, frightened shouting, other weapons answering, and in an instant he could hear the sounds of open warfare, rising through the shattered windows of LaMancha's room.

The Arab felt his stomach turning over. He knew he had walked into a trap.

Cursing, Rani pounded back along the hallway. He stumbled, but caught himself against the bannister. His pulse was hammering, hot breath rasping in his throat before he reached the lobby. Rani felt as if he might explode at any moment.

He had to join his men before it was too late.

Disgusted with himself, the Arab knew he might have already missed his chance.

10

In the blacksuit, Bolan had been crouching in a shadowed doorway opposite the Orient, the Beretta 93-R in its leather snug beneath his arm; the silver AutoMag, Big Thunder, rode his hip on military webbing. As his head weapon, Bolan had selected the lethal Uzi submachine gun. Hand grenades and extra magazines for all three weapons ringed his waist in O.D. canvas rigging.

He had waited for an hour in the shadows before the four-car caravan pulled in front of his hotel. A force of twenty soldiers piled out onto the street. Rani called his troops together on the curb, conversing with them briefly, rattling off some last-minute instructions. Bolan could not overhear his words but knew what he was saying. Considering the target, their strategy was obvious. They would bottle up the exits and dispatch a penetration team to bring their quarry out, alive or dead.

They had the numbers now, but Rani's timing was all wrong; his prey had already slipped out of the trap and doubled back on the enemy.

The hunters had become the hunted.

Rani's troops peeled off, some disappearing down an alley to the right of the hotel, others circling around the corner, moving out to plug the back door. Half a dozen took up station on the street beside the cars, an equal number followed Rani through the double doors.

Bolan knew the spearhead force would be upstairs in moments, ready to corral LaMancha in his lair, but they were in for a surprise.

The Executioner started counting, running down the numbers in his mind and waiting for the signal that his company had arrived. One hand found the radio-remote transceiver at his waist, beside the holstered AutoMag. Any moment now....

Rani's infantry was slack, undisciplined. As Bolan watched them, half the frontal force drifted off the mark, returned to the cars. Three of them climbed into a Fiat four-door and settled down to wait in comfort for their leader. Matches flared, and in another moment they were passing cigarettes around.

Waiting in the darkness, Bolan smiled. He could smell hashish. In ancient times, a band of murderers had used the drug to give themselves artificial courage, and these cutthroats—*hashashim*—had contributed the term "assassin" to the lexicon of mayhem. Bolan knew that hash and sentry duty were a lethal mixture for the user. He had seen enough of it in Nam, and the end results were always grisly.

At his waist, the miniature receiver chirped, a low metallic note announcing that the enemy had breached his door upstairs. Bolan keyed the detonator, sending a silent emissary beaming across the street to close the trap.

A brilliant flash of light, the muffled *crump* of the explosion, and his window shattered, spewing glass and masonry into the street below. The blast was followed by a ragged, choking scream. Flames leapt, rapidly consuming flesh and furnishings.

On the street, Rani's troops were startled from their torpor. Those still on foot were dodging through a rain of shattered glass and rubble, cursing, seeking cover from the deadly shower. The group of smokers in the Fiat were scrambling out of the car, shouting to their comrades on the curb, when Bolan launched his second-phase offensive.

On the driver's side of the Fiat, a lanky button man was hauling out a broom-handle Mauser from beneath his baggy jacket. Bolan took him with a short, precision Uzi-burst that picked the gunner off his feet and laid him out across the Fiat's hood. A tremor gripped the dying flesh, then stopped forever.

The troops were wide awake to danger, but uncertain of their enemy's position.

Concentrating on the crew beside the Fiat, Bolan drove them under cover with a probing burst, exploding safety glass into a thousand pebbled fragments. He was tracking on, the Uzi seeking other game before the enemy appeared to spot his sniper's nest.

A pair of soldiers spotted him, and they were moving in opposite directions, wrestling on the run with hidden hardware. Bolan chose the gunman to his left, the Uzi swinging smoothly into target acquisition. He was already squeezing off the deadly message when he found the man and held him in the submachine-gun's sights.

The Uzi shuddered; Bolan felt the lethal powers flowing through his arms and out the muzzle of his weapon. He could see the bullets shredding fabric, boring through in search of flesh and blood. A crimson torrent geysered out of the dying guncock.

The second gunner saw his partner die, and he faltered, frozen in his tracks. He had a pistol out, pumping lead in Bolan's general direction, but the rounds were going wide.

Bolan goosed the Uzi, rattling off a short burst at thirty yards. The gunner's skull exploded into bloody fragments. The Executioner tracked on in search of other hollow men.

Survivors huddling behind the Fiat were unlimbering their weapons, homing in on the Executioner. Hostile rounds were coming closer, snapping past him, chipping plaster overhead. One gunner had an assault rifle—a Kalashnikov, by the sound—and he was eating up the night around Bolan.

He huddled closer to the wall and held the Uzi's trigger down, 9mm bullets probing for a hot spot on the Fiat. He found it, and the fuel tank exploded thunderously, a ball of flame enveloping the squat Italian roadster. Bolan heard the gunners screaming as they fried.

A flaming gunman sprang and made his break, a human comet. Bolan let him go and concentrated on his own predicament. He prepared to make his move.

A lake of burning gasoline was spreading underneath the line of cars, and there were seconds left before they all went up in sequence. It was time to speed up the process. Bolan sprang a frag grenade from his harness, yanked the pin and let it fly with a soaring overhand delivery.

The deadly metal egg impacted on a fender, bounced once and exploded in the air, taking a dark sedan along with it. A second grenade was in the air before his first one detonated, and the stunning double blast consigned the string of vehicles to hell.

Bolan took advantage of the conflagration, breaking cover, firing as he ran. The Uzi emptied, and he ditched the useless magazine, feeding his stutter gun a fresh one on the run. Behind the dancing flames, survivors were intent on scrambling for safety, and the warrior stitched a line of parabellum manglers through the ranks to help them on their way. Some of them had reached the alley's mouth and were seeking sanctuary there when they collided with their reinforcements and were driven back into the battle zone.

Rani's flankers had arrived to join the carnage. Lured by the sounds of war, they stumbled into chaos and were momentarily dazed, unable to believe their eyes.

The Executioner announced his presence with a blazing figure eight that swept a pair of gunners off their feet. The others scattered, dodging off in all directions, pumping wild reflexive fire at any moving target. Stragglers were just arriving from the opposite direction, and the troops were firing at one another, frightened and disoriented.

Bolan crossed the fire-lighted no-man's-land with loping strides, shooting with a vengeance. One by one, the hostile guns were silenced, snipers falling prey to Bolan's sharp precision fire. A bloody moment longer, and the man in midnight black was moving through the killing ground alone.

He was alerted to Rani's presence when the tavern keeper stumbled down the hotel steps. He wore the look of a disaster victim, suddenly confronted by a scene beyond his comprehension. Bolan took advantage of the crew chief's temporary shock to put himself within arm's reach, edging up behind him like a shadow.

Rani jumped when Bolan pressed the muzzle of his chatter gun against one olive cheek. The Arab spun around, his Walther automatic jerking up and into shaky target acquisition, wavering on a level with the Phoenix warrior's waist. Bolan could have killed him when he moved, but he did not—that was not his plan.

Now they could kill each other. It would require a twitch of Rani's trigger finger, nothing more. A sudden-death exchange could end it all.

Bolan kept his voice low-key, almost a monotone. "It's up to you. Make your move."

Rani hesitated, then made his choice, dropping the Walther on the pavement.

Bolan brought the Uzi down against his side. "We haven't got a lot of time," he said. "Let's take it down the block."

Rani let himself be led along the street until they reached the alleyway. Gingerly, the Arab picked his way around a pair of riddled corpses, finally following Bolan into the shadows.

Bolan knew they were desperately short of time. Police would be responding swiftly. "You're marked," he told Rani. "Better find yourself a hole and crawl inside."

Rani looked bewildered, darting eyes a study in suspicion. "I don't understand."

Bolan feigned exasperation. "Put it all together. We were set up. Both of us."

"Set up?"

"Somebody wants me out of action. Two birds, one stone."

The Arab raised a hand, thought better of it and stuffed it in a pocket. He was anxious to be out of there, but he was tangled like a fly in Bolan's verbal web. "You speak in riddles."

"Someone has you marked expendable. Your ass is hanging out a mile."

"I have no enemies," the tavern keeper told him, bristling.

"Then you need a better class of friends. The ones you've got will eat you alive."

Rani dredged up the last of his nerve and challenged Bolan. "What are you doing in Algiers?"

"Like I told you, setting up a new connection, weeding out the old. Times are changing. Somebody doesn't like the signs."

Recognition dawned behind the Arab's eyes. "The war."

"It's in your own backyard. Better pick a winner while you can."

As if to stress the urgency of Bolan's words, a distant siren sounded, drawing nearer, joined immediately by another and another. Bolan saw the perspiration breaking out on Rani's face.

"You ask me to betray a trust."

"I'm giving you a chance to stay alive," he countered. "Your choice."

"I would require assurance...."

Bolan stopped him, pushing the Uzi's muzzle underneath the Arab's chin, forcing his head back. Rani swallowed hard, his Adam's apple colliding with the flash suppressor.

"You haven't got a thing to bargain with," Bolan told the thug. "Anyone I miss is coming after you."

"A shipment, scheduled for tonight," Rani stammered, giving in. "The *Liberté*, with cargo for the south. Everyone you want will be there."

"Time and place?"

The Arab rattled off an hour and the number of the freighter's berth. He was trembling now, with the sirens almost upon them, and Bolan knew he had pushed his captive to the limit.

"Live," he said. "Go find yourself that hole."

And he was moving out, abandoning the Arab. The Executioner had business to take care of—an unexpected shipment southward bound and only thirty minutes to prevent departure.

The game was slipping through his fingers, and he had to get it back before he lost it all. Perhaps, with any luck, he could take the sudden detour and convert it to a winning play.

Behind him, Bolan left a ticking time bomb of

his own. Rani was nursing doubts—about his place in the scum society, his superiors and the odds of his survival in Algiers. The soldier left him to it; whether Rani went to ground or ran to his employers was of little consequence. The damage had been done.

Divide and conquer, and let the opposition turn upon themselves, devour one another in a frenzy of suspicion while he chipped away at their defenses.

If it came to that.

If he could not take them all together in a single sweep.

Warrior Bolan melted into darkness, speeding toward a rendezvous with death along the waterfront.

11

Smiley Dublin checked her watch again and swore with feeling. Ten minutes down, and it felt like an hour. The walls of her sanctuary seemed to close around her, threatening her with claustrophobia.

Waiting was a pain, no doubt about it. Smiley knew the Bolan plan, and had willingly agreed to let him take the point on this oe, but the case was *hers*, dammit. There were enough enemies to go around, and she did not want to be frozen out entirely. Not when she had come so far and risked so much.

The Fed was all professional, tried and tested under fire. If Bolan expected her to step aside and take it easy while he fought her battles for her, he would have to think again. Bolan's life was interwoven with her life, his private war a logical extension of her own career at Sensitive Operations. When they met he was busy doing what the Feds had never found authority or courage to attempt: killing serpents, and scoring goals against the Mafia.

Smiley remembered Vegas and her meeting with Bolan. He had been a fugitive, already working on the title of Most Wanted Man Alive, hunted by Brognola and the other federal guns who would ally themselves with him in later battles. They had shared the killing grounds, and she had learned a thing or two about survival on the way to final victory in the green felt jungle.

There were other lessons in Hawaii, where a coalition of the Mafia and Chinese Communists were gathered for a ghoulish feast. They called the operation King Fire, and this time it was Smiley on the inside, challenging the savage coalition. Bolan had arrived as if by accident, following a game trail of his own. He had discovered Smiley—saved her bacon, if you got down to it—and together they had put the enemy down. King Fire had been consigned to hellfire.

After Honolulu, they had shared a fleeting moment of togetherness, restoring and renewing each other in the wake of mortal combat. Smiley would have liked a replay very much indeed, but her mind was on the mission now, computing angles, opportunities.

With Ben Battaglia, she had been inside the action. When she muffed it with her own over-confidence, the Executioner had pulled her out of yet another frying pan.... Now she was stuck on the outside again, looking in. Bolan had the ball, and she would have to find a way to get it back.

She recognized the soldier's absolute commitment to his war and admired him for it. Also, she felt a deep, abiding gratitude to Bolan for his understanding. He had never judged her for employing every trick and tool at her disposal to destroy the common enemy. To him, she was a fellow soldier and a valued ally—but, still, there was enough chivalry about the man that he endeavored to protect her from the heat, and that aroused a mixture of emotions in her.

Smiley finished pacing as she made the only possible decision. In a battle situation, soldiers did not wait for opportunities to come along; they made their own.

It was time for Smiley Dublin to start manufacturing some opportunities.

From Bolan, she knew all about the Arab, Rani and his Club Grandee. It was a starting point, at least, and she would play it by ear from there. If she struck out at Rani's, she could always double back and wait for Bolan. If she scored. . . .

Moving quickly, inspired with energy and zeal, she began a rapid transformation. She changed her clothes, emerging with a ''tourist look''—a little flashy and a little sexy, with a little conservatism sprinkled in. In her handbag, the compact Detonics .45 autoloader added weight and gave her a little extra confidence.

If needed, the minicannon would provide the awesome stopping power of its full-sized predecessors; but the woman was not looking for a firefight. Penetration was the play, and softly. She was after information, leads, not open confrontation.

The Phoenix safehouse was half a mile from Rani's turf inside the Casbah proper. Smiley flagged an ancient taxi at the curb and asked to be taken to the Club Grandee. The driver kept up a running monologue while weaving in and out of traffic, leaning on his horn at frequent intervals, berating other motorists and pedestrians in rapid gutter French. Smiley made the trip in silence, concentrating on her private thoughts.

The Club Grandee was everything she had expected. Seedy and dilapidated, with a clutch of ragged drunkards loitering outside, it was the archetype of every Middle Eastern dive she had ever heard or read about.

Smiley paid the driver and watched the taxi disappear. She was isolated, cut off behind the lines, but she kept her cool and confidence as she walked along the sidewalk, past a motley audience and through the entryway.

Inside, the air was thick with smoke. Tiny tables ringed an elevated stage where a hired dancer clad in harem garb was going through her paces, undulating rhythmically to flute and sitar. The patrons were predominantly male, though Smiley spotted several women in the crowd.

Smiley made her way across the packed floor, winding among the tables. Fast, groping hands scuttled out to brush against her thighs and buttocks as she passed. By the time she had run the gauntlet and found an empty bar stool, she craved a long hot shower.

Behind the bar, a very tall man with a jagged scar across his cheek was sliding over to take her order. His eyes devoured her, lingering on her breasts, and Smiley felt involuntary color rising in her cheeks. Determined not to let it show, she leaned toward him and raised her voice to make it heard above the music.

"Hi. You Rani?"

"Rani's gone. Drink?"

"I really need to see your boss."

Scar tissue crinkled as the Tuareg frowned. "Gone."

"Well, then, I'll have a glass of wine. . .and wait."

The shrug was almost too casual. Scarface moved away from her along the bar and returned a moment later with a brimming glass of wine. Smiley paid him, took a sip, and made a sour face at his retreating back. The wine was sickly sweet, and it left an oily feeling in her mouth. She wondered if the glasses were ever washed.

Killing time, she swiveled on her stool to watch

the dancer. Young and shapely, she was trying to inject a semblance of emotion into what was obviously a tedious routine. Every dip and turn was well rehearsed, almost mechanical, and Smiley half expected her to yawn at any moment. The face was that of someone who has seen and heard it all before.

Droning, tinny music and the smoky atmosphere were having their effect on Smiley. Watching as the dancer spun in front of her, she felt a creeping dizziness invade her body. She took another swallow of her wine and found the taste remarkably improved.

Unexpectedly, the lanky Tuareg was beside her, leaning close. Rancid breath enveloped her as he began to speak.

"You come with me."

"I beg your pardon?"

"Rani say you come."

Smiley felt a quickening of the pulse. She drained her glass and followed him along the bar on shaky legs. For a single second, the room appeared to tilt, and she braced herself against the wine's surprising kick. She cursed herself for ordering the drink and bit her lower lip, welcoming the pain that briefly cleared her head.

The Tuareg led her through a beaded curtain, then down a narrow, grimy corridor illuminated by weak bulbs at either end. Trailing him, she slipped a hand inside her shoulder bag and found the small Detonics .45. She wrapped her fist around its reassuring form.

Smiley did not intend to let herself be taken by surprise.

At the end of the corridor, her guide opened a wooden door and stood aside to let her pass. She edged past him, had the time to register a room beyond the door, then the Tuareg struck her with an open palm between the shoulder blades, propelling her across the little office.

Smiley stumbled, gasping, momentarily out of breath. She caught her balance and spun around to face her enemy. Her ears were ringing, and her vision was blurred; she recognized the drug's effects and again cursed her carelessness.

She had let her guard down momentarily, left herself wide open, and now she was paying for it.

Smiley ripped the automatic from her purse and thrust it toward her lumbering attacker. He was on top of her before she could release the safety catch; she squeezed the trigger ineffectually. The Tuareg swatted it away, a numbing blow that left her hand and forearm tingling. She heard the pistol clatter onto tile. There was no chance of recovering it in time.

The Tuareg was boring in relentlessly, blocking the knee she aimed at his groin, delivering a slashing backhand blow across her face. Blinding pain exploded in her skull, and Smiley lost her balance, sprawling onto the floor. She tried to wriggle out of reach, but he was after her at once, grappling with her, pinning both her arms against her sides.

She tried the knee again, connected with his ribs and heard the breath rush out of him. He cursed in Arabic, and then a huge fist impacted on her cheek with savage force.

Smiley collapsed, surrendering to the pain, her mind a jumble of disjointed sights and sounds. Above her, the bartender's face was badly out of focus, divided by a heartless smile. She felt his hands upon her, and she tried to struggle. She could not move.

He frisked her thoroughly for other weapons, callused fingers probing every part of her, lingering here and there. Revulsion mingled with pain, but there was no escape. Another moment, and the Tuareg hauled her to her feet, lifted her without apparent effort, folded her across his shoulder in a fireman's carry.

Thus inverted, fading in and out of consciousness, Smiley was borne across the office. At the far wall, her captor tripped a hidden switch and waited while a massive cabinet revolved on its hidden axis. A wave of musty air invited them inside the tunnel.

Smiley had a sick sensation of descending into hell. The man-made cavern's claustrophobic atmosphere was dank and foul, heavy with the smell of rot and rodents. As the Tuareg carried her along through darkness, she could hear the chattering of startled rats, the scrabble of their claws on hard-packed soil. She felt the contents of her stomach rolling, rising, and then the strangling darkness swallowed her alive.

12

Mack Bolan huddled in the shadow of an empty warehouse and scrutinized the *Liberté*. Fifty yards away, the freighter rode a gentle swell, her barnacle-encrusted hull grating against the pier.

Moonlight bathed the waterfront. Centuries of lovers might have found the setting romantic, but Phoenix saw it all in tactical relation to his mission. Moonlight was treacherous, a beacon to expose his presence.

The *Liberté* was an aging tramp. The ship showed her years like an ancient whore who lacked the energy to paint her face. Constructed in the wake of global war, she must have passed through many hands; the new Liberian registry concealed her current ownership.

But Bolan had no interest in the freighter's pedigree. He already knew enough to condemn her. But there was a job to do, precautions to be taken before he brought the curtain down.

The vessel was a slaver, and he did not ignore the irony of her name. Crouching in the darkness, he wondered how much human cargo she had carried, how many weapons and narcotics shipments.

Too damn many, he thought.

Bolan had expected more activity around the ship, and he was on alert, suspicious of the brooding silence. On the freighter's bridge, a light was visible, and he picked out sporadic movement on the decks, but there was nothing of the bustle that precedes a sailing. If the *Liberté* was outward bound tonight, she hid it well.

He considered whether Rani might have set him up, and just as quickly abandoned the thought. The Arab had been terrified, dealing for his life. Bolan did not read him as a man adept at fabricating stories under stress. He was tough and sharp enough when he was in control, but when a gun was pointed at his head. . . .

Bolan knew he would have to find his answers on the *Liberté*, nowhere else.

And his biggest problem was finding a way on board without alerting anxious sentries.

The gangplank was still in place, apparently unguarded, but the man in black was not about to risk an entry by the front door. There were other ways to skin the viper, and Bolan had his angles calculated long before he gave up the safety of the shadows for open ground.

The soldier made it to the ship in a sprint, crossing forty yards of asphalt and ten yards of weathered planking in a little less than seven seconds. Deeper shadows welcomed him along the pier, and he used another moment to let his pulse and respiration stabilize before proceeding with his penetration.

If there were sentries waiting topside, they would be watching for intruders on the gangplank. Bolan opted for the berthing hawser and a scramble to the fantail, twenty feet above his head. It was a risk, of course, but the alternative was almost certain death.

With the Uzi slung across his shoulder, Bolan wriggled up the mooring line hand over hand, working cautiously around the ratcatchers strung a dozen feet apart. He reached the hawsehole, got a leg up and vaulted lightly over the rusty railing to the afterdeck.

He was not alone.

Bolan felt the danger before he knew its source. A lookout, revolver angled through his belt, was gaping in alarm. The guy was not expecting company, but he recovered quickly, clutching at his gun as he hit a fighting crouch. Professional, and almost fast enough to pull it off.

Bolan never let him reach the weapon. As the nightfighter hit the deck, he had the silent-death Beretta in his fist. By the time he saw his adversary, Bolan's pistol had acquired the target, trigger finger already tightening into the squeeze.

The weapon chugged, and a parabellum bone-crusher closed the gap between them, punching between the lookout's startled eyes, boring on to find the brain within. Lifeless fingers froze around the butt of the guard's revolver, and he toppled forward on his face, a scarecrow with the stuffing knocked out.

Bolan sheathed his 93-R and moved to where the guy was sprawled across the deck. He carried the lookout to the railing, and he slid the limp body over into darkness, waiting for the splash of impact. When he was alone, the warrior moved on in search of answers to many deadly questions.

A circuit of the upper decks, avoiding seamen when they crossed his path, showed him nothing out of the ordinary for a ship in port. Probing farther, Bolan found an open hatch. He scrambled down the metal stairway into darkness, finding his way with a pencil flash. He palmed the Beretta, ready to respond to any challenge.

There was nothing in the cabins, nothing in the cargo hold.

Nothing.

The penetration was a washout.

Bolan put his mind to work on possibilities, alternatives. The tavern keeper could have lied to him, of course, but that still seemed unlikely. It was also improbable that Rani would mistake the ship's departure time. Only one logical alternative remained: the shipment had been scheduled as described, and then postponed or cancelled without Rani's knowledge.

That left the operation pending, and the human cargo still in jeopardy. Bolan would have to find them and release them from their bondage. If the answers he sought were on the *Liberté*, he would find them on the bridge, but first there were some doomsday preparations to be made.

Bolan retraced his steps, pausing at strategic points along the way to mold plastic charges to the hull. From an O.D. canvas pouch, he drew the radio-remote detonators, wedging them in place by feel, not relying on the flash.

A signal from the tiny detonator box attached to Bolan's web belt would trigger all the charges, simultaneously or in any sequence he chose. He had come to sink a slaver, and that he would do—but the soldier's job was not completed. There was one more stop to make before he started burning bridges.

Colonel Phoenix had a date with the captain of the *Liberté*. And it was time to pull some rank in old Algiers.

He gained the deck and moved along through mottled moonlight toward the wheelhouse. Twice he had to pause and seek the shelter of a shadowed doorway, keeping out of sight as crewmen went about their jobs. No one marked his passage toward the stairs.

Bolan took the steps two at a time, approaching from the blind side of anybody on the bridge, and in another moment he was with them, uninvited Death appearing at the captain's table.

There were two men in the wheelhouse, and Bolan sized them up at once. He marked the older one, a swarthy, balding man, as skipper of the *Liberté*. His young companion wore a uniform, and Bolan caught the telltale bulge of holstered hardware underneath his arm.

Phoenix stepped inside the wheelhouse and rapped the muzzle of his Beretta against the door to announce himself. Two startled faces turned to gape at him, the older man going pale, the younger going mean.

And in the different reactions, Bolan read their fates, as clearly as a surgeon reads his patient's vital signs. The younger officer was eager for a fight, and in his confidence he never stopped to weigh the odds against him. His hand was streaking for the hidden gun before his captain could restrain him.

Bolan had the slim Beretta set for automatic fire. He nudged the trigger, let a rapid three-round burst declare his purpose. Parabellum manglers drilled precisely on the mark, punching him backward and across the captain's chart table. Half a dozen maps were taken with him to the floor, and those he left behind were stained with seeping blood.

He had the captain's full attention now. The guy was standing, studying the scene of carnage with disbelieving eyes—gaping first at Bolan and his smoking weapon, then at his riddled mate, then back to the black-clad messenger of death.

"English?" Bolan snapped.

The captain nodded, a jerky motion.

"You booked a shipment for tonight. I'm here to take delivery."

The skipper hesitated, a curtain falling into place behind the nervous eyes. "No shipment here. All empty."

Bolan closed the gap between them, jammed the muzzle of his silencer against a flabby cheek. The metal was still warm from firing, and the cheek began to twitch, but its owner did not dare pull away.

"One last time," the soldier growled. "I'm looking for your cargo."

Something snapped inside the pudgy sailor. "Everything is gone, effendi. All the women. . . ."

"When and where?"

The skipper missed the question. He was on a roll, desperate to persuade the soldier of his innocence. "Armand has cancelled everything," he blurted out. "No more business now."

"Why not?"

"There is a spy. . . a woman. Armand tells me

there may be others. No more business now until he can find out."

Faint alarm bells were sounding in the back of Bolan's mind; a heavy lump was forming in his stomach. "This spy, where was she captured? Where have they taken her?"

The skipper tried to shake his head, but Bolan's weapon prevented him. Beads of sweat were glistening on his forehead. "Please," he whispered. "I have told you everything. Armand does not explain."

Bolan tried another line. "I need to find the other women. Where are they kept?"

A strangled squeal escaped from the captain's throat before he found his voice again. "I do not *know*. The Corsican, his friends, they do not confide in anyone."

His words had the ring of truth, and Bolan eased his pressure on the slim Beretta's trigger. Stepping back a pace, he gave the captain room to breathe. "Better hit the panic button, give your crew a running start," he said. "You're sinking."

Confusion mingled with panic on the skipper's face as he attempted to decipher Bolan's words. He glanced around him, spotted nothing out of place, and finally found the nerve to address the nightfighter. "I do not understand."

In lieu of answer, Bolan dropped his free hand to waist level and found the miniature transceiver by touch. He tripped a preselected switch, dispatching an urgent message to the stern, away from their position.

The captain understood Bolan when the hollow thunder of a blast below decks shook the *Liberté*. The ancient tramp was listing, already sinking by the stern before Mack Bolan reached the entrance to the bridge.

Behind him, the captain was scrambling for the intercom, setting off alarms and shouting orders over the PA system, his static-laden voice competing with the shouting from below. There was something in his voice that made Bolan turn around and glance at him in parting.

The captain's nerve had finally broken. He was weeping now, openly and unashamedly. The guy could feel his life collapsing, sinking under him, and at the moment there was nothing he could do but watch it happen.

The Executioner could feel no pity for the skipper of the *Liberté*.

Almost.

But he remembered that the sailor was a cannibal at heart, and undeserving of his pity. The man had climbed in bed with savages and let them use him for a price. He had carried helpless women into bondage, ferried arms and cruel narcotics that annihilated thousands.

He had sold his soul, and in its place there was a dark malignancy, potentially contagious.

Only righteous fire could wipe the stain away, prevent a foul proliferation.

Bolan reached the stairs and started down. Below, a pair of hostile guns came into view. They were coming up on the run, apparently unaware of his presence, preoccupied with other problems and intent on speaking to the captain. By the time they recognized their danger, it was too late to take effective action.

Bolan stitched them with the 93-R, left to right and back again, then vaulted over crumpled bodies, grasping at his detonator as he reached the deck.

The freighter trembled, rocked beneath a second blast, and a tongue of flame sprang upward from the forward cargo hold. Smoke and steam were rising from below deck, curling up through open ports and hatches, creating a hellish fog.

Bolan used the smoke screen to his advantage, brushing past the frightened guards and seamen, undetected in the general confusion. Homing on the gangplank, he made it through and found the way predictably unguarded. Anyone on duty when the charges detonated would be busy hauling ass to save himself.

A dozen loping strides and he was on the pier, retreating into darkness while the freighter burned behind him. Angry shouting gave way to screams, and now the flames were running free, out of control.

He keyed the final switch and was waiting when another explosion hit the *Liberté* amidships. Before his eyes the freighter seemed to roll, the decks canting drastically, disgorging men and loose equipment into rolling water. Sliding lower, the ship was grinding against the pier. Sailors were trapped against the dock, screaming helplessly beneath the juggernaut.

Bolan closed his mind to all of it and turned away. He had a more immediate concern, compelling him to action, demanding an immediate solution.

He had missed his target on the waterfront. The human cargo had been whisked away. He could never rest until they were recovered safely or avenged.

Also, the slavers had unearthed a spy whose disclosure made them seek the shadows, go to ground. Already, Bolan might have missed his shot at a conclusive sweep of the Algerian operation.

But it was the latest captive who disturbed him most of all. His gut told him it must be Smiley Dublin. He would have to check it out before proceeding any further.

He was returning to the safehouse, racing against the clock. Bolan prayed that Smiley would be there to greet him—but he knew with chilling certainty that she would not be.

13

When he reached the safehouse, Bolan made a cautious drive-by, circling the block, taking time to scrutinize pedestrians and vehicles parked against the curb. His combat sensors probed the night, searching for any sign of danger, any thing or person that might betray an ambush. If Smiley had been taken, security was breached, and he was on his own. The enemy could surface anywhere, at any time.

He was back in the jungle, with all the laws of brute survival in effect. It was kill or be killed.

He made the circuit, parked his Audi in the narrow alleyway adjacent and prepared to take the back entrance.

The Executioner moved up a single flight of stairs and then along a dimly lighted corridor, reaching the small apartment without incident. Mindful of the sabotage potential, he spent a moment at the door, listening for any sound inside, examining the knob and frame for signs of tampering. When he was satisfied it had not been wired, he used his extra key and slipped inside, the black Beretta ready in his fist.

It took only a second to see the place was empty. Smiley had been there, but she was gone.

He returned the pistol to its armpit sheath and set about examining the drop, attempting to discover something...anything at all that could put him on her trail.

There was no sign of struggle, nothing that would indicate hostile penetration. Based on the evidence, Smiley had departed willingly, for reasons of her own.

Momentary anger and exasperation flared inside Bolan, and he cursed the Fed for her stubbornness.

Smiley could be anywhere—she could be dead. Bolan put the thought away from him at once; the skipper of the *Liberté* had been persuasive in his story that "the spy" was still alive.

"There is a spy...a woman."

That implied a living captive, and the mastermind of slavery in Algiers would be unlikely to dispose of her without exhausting his interrogation methods.

Bolan felt his stomach turning over, rolling, as unbidden memories came flooding back— memories of butchered humans, tortured by the Mafia's professional inquisitors, clinging pointlessly to life after sanity had fled.

The vermin in North Africa would have refinements of their own for jarring stubborn memories and loosening tongues. If Smiley was in hostile hands. . . .

The warrior cursed again, and now, in place of nausea, a white-hot rage was building inside him. He would have to act swiftly if there was any hope of saving Smiley. He had a list of targets that might hold the key to her whereabouts. With such a slate to choose from, the Executioner in fact had very little choice.

He would attack them all.

A blitz in old Algiers, and somewhere along the way he would jar loose the crucial information that he needed—or he would die in the attempt.

The tactic had worked for him in other wars.

Swiftly, unemotionally, he started making preparations for the new offensive, choosing weapons and munitions with the care a surgeon shows in selecting instruments. Darkness covered Bolan on his two trips to the car, descending narrow stairs with heavy O.D. duffel bags on either shoulder. He would not leave anything behind that could later identify him.

The Audi would be serving as his mobile operations base until he found Smiley or until the enemy shot it out from under him—whichever came first. It was time to move.

The doomsday fuse was lighted and burning

fiercely in Algiers. In the wake of that apocalyptic blast, there would be nothing left unchanged.

The Executioner was blitzing on.

SMILEY DUBLIN struggled in the darkness, battling against a running tide. Her arms were weighted, legs numb, paralytic. The current sucked her back into the black void. She felt as if she were drowning.

Consciousness had returned to Smiley by degrees. She became aware at first of small sounds competing with the rhythm of her pulse, then the darkness was retreating, giving way to painful light. When she opened her eyes, the pain was dazzling, but brief. Her mouth was dry, as if she had been chewing cotton in her sleep. Smiley recognized the sour aftertaste of medication.

She had been sedated.

With consciousness, her memory returned, the circuits clicking into place, imagination filling in the gaps. The scar-faced bartender had spiked her drink, and Smiley knew he could have made the dose a lethal one. She was alive, and that meant someone wanted her that way.

The thought was something less than comforting.

Smiley was seated on a wooden chair, wrists and ankles tightly bound with leather straps. She tried to rock the chair from side to side, but its legs were set too far apart, and she eventually gave up. Since she clearly was immobilized, Smiley set about establishing where she was.

Around her, walls of native stone ascended from the concrete floor to plaster ceiling without sign of doors or windows. Any entrance to the room had to be behind her. She had no clear impression of the size of the room. The temperature and dampness told her the chamber was a basement of some sort. A *dungeon*, from all appearances.

In front of her, the wall was fitted with manacles, and there were other grim accoutrements, both antique and modern. Some of the torture implements reminded Smiley of mementos from the Spanish Inquisition.

Her captors had an eye for lethal hardware. Smiley wondered how they were at putting it to use, and she was sickened by the images that came to mind. She found herself remembering Georgette Chableu with fear instead of customary sadness.

Danger was a fact of life for every agent in the field, but there were degrees of savagery at which the mind rebelled. Smiley had prepared herself for violent death, but she hoped it would be quick and clean—a righteous soldier going down with all guns blazing.

Her helplessness was stifling, and Smiley felt on the verge of tears. Silently, she cursed herself for weakness in the face of peril, for allowing this to happen in the first place. Twice she had been captured while working on the same case. She was angered by her own overanxiousness, over-aggressiveness.

Now, she had a single grim priority: survival.

If escape was possible, she had to find the way. If not, she would keep the Bolan secret and wait for him to find her, take her out of there.

And he would come for her in time. He had to.

A heavy door opened and closed again behind her. Someone was approaching on her blind side, circling to the left. She registered a single set of footsteps on concrete, but three figures suddenly appeared.

At a glance, they were a clownish trio. The central figure, obviously in control, was a slender woman decked out in black leather vest and shorts, with fishnet hose to match. Her reddish hair was cut short, a mannish style that made her face look angular and hard. Smiley placed her in her mid-forties.

The flankers were a matching pair of giants chiseled out of ebony. They were dressed as harem guards, complete with baggy trousers and turbans wrapped around their heads. Each of them was nearly seven feet in height, and they were built like Olympic weight lifters. Broad, flat faces were devoid of any emotion.

Under other circumstances, Smiley might

have burst out laughing at the image they presented, but here and now, the overall effect was frightening.

She did her best to keep from staring, but the woman in leather seemed to read her mind. When she spoke, Smiley marked the German accent, scarcely softened by a life abroad.

"Genuine eunuchs," the woman offered conversationally. "They are expensive, but amusing."

Smiley read a chilling sadism in the voice, but she kept cool and countered with a question of her own. "What am I doing here?"

Her captor smiled. Her face held no feeling. "Ah," she purred. "The crucial question. You anticipate me."

Smiley did not have to feign the rising anger that she felt. "I was drugged and carried here against my will," she snapped. "Now I *demand* to know exactly where I am and what the hell is going on."

Her jailer faked a curtsy, clapped her hands together in appreciation. "Excellent. An admirable performance, *liebchen*. Worthy of an award." The face and voice reverted to stone. "Now, *bitch*, I ask the questions and you give the answers. Understood?"

Smiley matched the Arctic tone. "Go to hell."

The woman stiffened, clenching her fists in

white-knuckled fury. It required another moment for her voice to surface. "You are trying my patience. There is a limit. You will tell me, now, your business at Club Grandee. Why do you seek the owner? Spy duty?"

Thinking fast, Smiley tried to bluff it out.

"Rani? I heard on the street that he was the man to see about connections here in town."

"Connections?"

"Right. You know—a little hash, a little blow, nothing heavy. Look, if you guys are drug enforcement...."

The laugh was harsh, explosive. "How delightful. I admire your talent for improvisation. Now, I ask you once again: what is your business in Algiers?"

"I already told you, dammit."

The open-handed blow was stunning. Smiley's ears were ringing. She felt a rivulet of blood escape her nostril and dribble down across her lips and chin. She kept her voice rigid, swallowing her rage. "I want to see the American consul."

This time she saw it coming, bracing herself before the blow impacted on her cheek. The German wore a heavy ring, and it opened up a ragged gash beneath her eye, releasing a stream of blood.

"You are becoming tedious," her captor sneered. "I have the means to make you speak.

Before I finish, you will manufacture information, anything at all to stop the pain.''

A sudden chill invaded Smiley's bones, raising gooseflesh along her arms and lifting hair on the back of her neck. She shrugged it off and tried to match the firmness of the German's tone.

''Go to hell,'' she said again.

The smile was mocking now. ''I thought you understood, my dear. We are already there.''

Smiley Dublin closed her eyes and swallowed down her rising bile. In her mind, she saw Georgette again, the precious, tortured face transforming, twisting into yet another countenance. . . until it became her own.

14

Ali ibn-Hassan stood in darkness, listening to the muted whirring of the camera. Beyond a pane of mirrored one-way glass, naked bodies tangled on a giant oval bed. The Arab watched them closely, missing nothing, as the camera captured every movement, preserving it all on tape.

Two of the performers were professionals, the third a zealous amateur, completely unaware that he was being captured for posterity. Hassan admired his stamina, but there was still a certain clumsiness about his methods—a deliberate awkwardness that verged on the brutal.

Ali smiled, reflecting that he could expect no better from a police captain. The man was more familiar with inflicting pain than pleasure, more at home with violence than passion.

Technique was unimportant to the overall effect. He had the captain's face on tape, and that was all that mattered.

Ali's secret window was one of several, all strategically positioned in a suite designed for sexual games. He kept the room for special customers, those who could afford his prices—now and later. Patrons who could help him with his business, keep it running smoothly, turning in a handsome profit, were often blackmailed with the tapes, a most effective bargaining device.

The Arab's mind was drifting, and he found it difficult to concentrate on the captain and his energetic playmates. Other matters were commanding his attention. He had heard street rumors and had received the urgent message from Armand demanding that he shut down operations. Armand had offered nothing in the way of explanations, but Hassan had heard enough from his own sources to put some pieces of the puzzle in place.

He knew, for example, that a battle had erupted at the Orient hotel that very evening. A dozen independent guns were dead and authorities still picking through the wreckage for a clue to what had started it. And there were other unconfirmed stories of a shooting at Armand's château in el-Biar.

Something was happening, but what?

Ali refused to worry at the moment. His relations with Armand were common knowledge on the street—the Corsican was supplying him with women and drugs—but he retained a fair degree of personal autonomy. He had stayed away from the other side of Armand's operation—the sale of arms and women out of the country, trafficking with certain terrorists. The company Dusault was keeping lately made him feel uneasy, vaguely threatened, and the recent violence came to him as no surprise.

Hassan preferred to bide his time, building a stable base of power and quietly recruiting troops. Someday, perhaps a good deal sooner than expected, Armand's leadership position would be vacant.

And Ali had himself in mind as the Corsican's replacement. He thought he was ready for the upward move.

Above all else, he was not closing down his lavish pleasure palace just because Armand had ordered it. Hassan could not afford to turn away wealthy tourists or his local regulars.

Beyond the glass, the captain spent himself at last, displaying a final grimace for the hidden camera before collapsing into satin sheets.

The Arab checked his watch and saw that it was time to make his evening rounds. He was not expecting trouble, but he liked to make a nightly appearance. It cemented Ali's friendship with his regulars and kept them coming back.

He left the camera running, just in case the captain found his second wind and made the tape into a double feature. Hassan left the hidden room adjacent to his private office, moving briskly down a narrow hallway toward the stairs. He was on the landing, starting down, when all hell broke loose below.

A thunderclap destroyed the giant double doors at the front of the building and filled the entryway with smoke. A dozen of his girls were screaming, a couple of his patrons cursing loudly. Behind him, the bedroom doors were springing open in a rapid-fire reaction to the downstairs blast.

Hassan recovered from his shock, and he was moving down the staircase when a man dressed in nightfighter black suddenly materialized below. The fighter had weapons dangling from a military belt and harness, and in his hands he held a weapon that reminded Ali of a cross between a cannon and a Thompson submachine gun—big and shiny, equipped with a circular drum magazine. When the weapon swung in his direction, Ali thought the muzzle looked about the size of a forty-gallon oil drum.

A wasted lifetime flashed before the Arab's eyes, and he was struggling with the words to a forgotten prayer when circumstance provided a reprieve. Two of his soldiers, responding to the blast, appeared below him, weapons drawn, searching for a target.

The intruder saw them coming and spun to face them. His impressive weapon bellowed, bucked, and downrange the charging gunmen were enveloped by a ball of fire. The concussions shattered glassware, flattened Ali on the stairs, and suddenly the air was full of singing shrapnel.

Hassan scrambled back up the stairs. The man in black was leveling his pleasure palace, firing off selected rounds of colored smoke and choking gas. Blind and gagging, Ali found the landing with his groping hands and pulled himself erect with the aid of the bannister.

Armand had caused this, brought this plague of violence on his house. He had offended someone, militants or Mafia, and now there was a war in old Algiers. Hassan would kill the Corsican. . . if he survived to get the chance.

A naked body slammed against him on the run, and Ali recognized the captain's cursing voice. The brothel keeper staggered and caught himself against the railing.

A new explosion punched a hole through the clouds, and for a second Ali saw the man in midnight black below him, awesome weapon angled skyward. Flame erupted from the muzzle, and Hassan could *see* the black projectile hurtling toward him.

Ali became airborne, plummeting, a screaming cartwheel terminated by his impact on a heavy wooden table. It collapsed beneath his weight, and then the sky fell, wood and stone and plaster raining down on top of him. Something landed with a crushing weight across his legs, and savage pain forced him to scream.

In a moment, the man in black was standing over him, a grim colossus with his silver weapon leveled at the Arab's face. His lips were moving, but it took another second for Ali to register his words and translate from English.

"I want the woman," he was snarling. "Somebody knows where she is. Spread the word."

Ali ibn-Hassan closed his eyes, half expecting fiery death to issue from the cannon and consume him. Nothing happened. He dared another glance and discovered his enemy had disappeared. He was alone.

The brothel keeper tried to move his legs and found them twisted, pinned against the floor. He started screaming for his houseman, anyone who could help him.

Ali had to find a doctor and relieve the agony that racked his lower body. Then, when he was patched together, he had a call to make—a score to settle with Armand.

MACK BOLAN crouched on a sloping roof, his combat senses probing at the night. Middle-class Algiers was spread below him—lighted shops and homes, people going about their business in the streets, unaware of Grim Death poised above their heads.

The soldier was preparing for another strike, his third in less than two hours. Already he had trashed a fashionable brothel and destroyed a powder factory in the Casbah, keeping on the move and leaving word whenever he touched down. By now the message would be traveling like wildfire around the city. Someone would be squirming from the heat.

And the Executioner was far from finished.

Two floors below him, in a third-story suite of offices, were the local headquarters for an active terrorist group, the Palestinian People's Army. Pulled together from the ranks of PLO defectors and survivors of the Black September gang, the PPA lately had taken credit for a string of bombings on the Continent, a pair of bloody border raids on the Israeli frontier.

They were on the Bolan hit parade—especially since he discovered that their weapons and munitions were supplied by Armand Dusault.

Dusault was also on the warrior's list, but not until later. Any premature move he made against the top gun could rebound against him, against Smiley.

He preferred to touch the bases, keep the pressure building toward a flashpoint.

He secured the black nylon rope to a metal vent, tested it against his weight, and dropped the coil over the edge of the roof into freefall. Another moment to adjust his combat harness, double-check his weapons, and the warrior followed it down.

His target was a lighted window halfway

down the building's stucco face. Inside, a group of Palestinian guerrillas were discussing strategy.

Bolan scrambled down the wall until he found a vantage point beside the target window. Craning to his right, he could observe the terrorist commandos, grouped around a table littered with assorted books and papers. All of them were armed, and he spied a pair of gunners seated by the doorway with automatic rifles in their laps.

Bolan eased the safety off his Uzi submachine gun and braced himself against the wall. If he used the slim advantage of surprise to balance out their numbers and their guns, he had a chance.

The nightfighter pushed off, springing away from the wall and swinging in on target like a human pendulum. Outstretched feet impacted on the glass and as the pane shattered, Bolan slipped the quick-release latch on his climbing rig, hurtled through the window and landed in a fighting crouch.

The Palestinians were turning, startled, gaping at him. The quicker men were scrambling for weapons when the soldier opened fire. He took the doorway gunners first, pinning them to the wall with a deadly figure eight, the parabellum manglers shredding flesh and bone, drilling through to stitch a bloody pattern on the plaster.

Sweeping on, he held the Uzi's trigger down and sprayed the table. Men were diving, dying. A headless figure sprawled across the tabletop. Bolan watched it flopping like a mackeral out of water.

On his flank, another pair of riflemen erupted from a hidden alcove, Kalashnikov assault rifles tracking onto target. Bolan met them with a pair of short, precision bursts that blew them both away.

At his back, a wooden chair overturned, clattering to the floor. Bolan pivoted to meet the final threat, prepared to kill, and found himself confronted by a slender figure with one arm held aloft, the bloody ruin of his other held against his side.

Bolan recognized the face from news reports and briefings at Stony Man Farm. A former aide to Yasser Arafat and crony of the Black Septemberists, this man was a radical, perpetually in pursuit of some group willing to espouse his own beliefs. Of late, he had found refuge in the army of his own creation.

Through his shock, the guy was struggling to speak. Bolan took the initiative away from him, crossing the room in four long strides, jamming the Uzi's muzzle between his moving lips. He let the Arab taste it, feel the heat against his lips and tongue before he spoke.

"Listen like your life depends on it," he

snapped, watching the terrorist's eyes. "I'm looking for the woman. Anything that's going down with her better be called off, or there'll be hell to pay."

He did not expect an answer, and he did not wait around for one. Moving softly, cautiously, he put that place behind him, already thinking toward his next target zone.

The heat was rising in Algiers, and someone would be screaming soon. In time, the Corsican would hear those screams in el-Biar, and he would have to listen.

They would be among the final sounds he ever heard.

ARMAND DUSAULT cradled the telephone, released his breath in a weary sigh. A headache was throbbing just above his eyes, and he felt a sour burning in his stomach. Both were symptomatic of the tension that had plagued him since the afternoon, and there was no relief in sight.

By all accounts, Algiers was burning down around him, hungry flames endangering an empire that had taken years to build. Demands for aid were pouring in from every quarter, but Armand himself was groping in the dark, without a solid handle on the situation.

Someone had declared a shooting war on his preserve, but the Corsican was ignorant of motives and objectives, even the identity of his assailants. And their tactics. . . .

Half a dozen lightning thrusts had taken place—at the brothel of Ali ibn-Hassan, a warehouse used for holding contraband, the transport *Liberté* at dockside. An excellent heroin-processing plant had been reduced to smoking ashes, and explosive charges had destroyed a fleet of trucks belonging to an influential *mafioso*.

The latest call for help had come from Jamal Haddad, fiery organizer of the Palestinian People's Army. Several of his men were dead, their office wrecked, and Jamal himself had been wounded in an armed invasion of the PPA's clandestine headquarters. Like the rest, Haddad was an associate—and he demanded action from Armand. Something, anything to ease the heat.

The Corsican was fresh out of solutions. In fact, he was still working on a definition of the problem.

Stories from the trenches were remarkably consistent: a single awesome warrior, dressed in black, appeared and disappeared at will, leaving death and ruin in his wake. Everywhere he struck there was a message left behind with the survivors, something cryptic and oblique. . . about a woman he was seeking.

It was eerie, frightening—and all the more infuriating since Armand had no idea what his enemy was talking about.

Logic told Dusault there must be other foes at large, a body of supporting troops, but they were hanging back, allowing one commando to spearhead their assault.

If it *was* a single man. . . .

Armand was not convinced. The plague of violence was premeditated, well rehearsed. It had a military flavor reminiscent of the OAS and Legionnaires, as if a band of militants had chosen his Algiers to be their testing ground.

Except that Armand, a prime supplier of weapons and munitions, was friendly with the local militants. He had taken time to cultivate the terrorists for allies; they would not turn against him without a reason, on a whim.

He needed time to think, without the constant pressure and the nagging phone calls. Every moment that he wasted the faceless enemy was gaining ground.

Armand decided it was time to share the burden, just as he shared the profits from his empire. He would summon Mustaffa and the countess, force them each to shoulder part of the responsibility and risk.

It was time for the not-so-silent partners to express themselves. If necessary, they could take up arms to help defend the mutual investment.

That decision made, Armand felt a measure of the tension draining out of him. He snared the telephone receiver, started dialing. He would have them both in el-Biar within the hour, laying out a strategy.

And he could turn the lightning war around, with courage, systematic ruthlessness, determination. Armand was prepared to wrest the initiative from his opponents and ram it down their screaming throats.

In a struggle to the death, Armand Dusault would be victorious. He knew it.

It was his destiny.

15

On his second visit, Bolan scarcely recognized the Club Grandee. In place of crowds and joviality, the bar was shuttered, darkened, hours before closing time. A rapid recon of the neighborhood had put the soldier's mind at ease concerning traps.

From his vantage point across the street, the Executioner was watching as a pair of black Mercedes tanks pulled up in front. Doors opened, gunners scrambled out and formed a rough phalanx along the curb.

Bolan knew he was not looking at an honor guard. Somebody wanted Rani badly enough to send a double crew for him, and the way they were flourishing the hardware, he might not be scheduled to go back with them alive.

Someone—perhaps the Corsican, Armand—was burning bridges, settling with Rani for the Orient hotel debacle. Given the events of hours past, it was inevitable.

The drivers hung back, staying with their vehicles while the strike force, about seven guns in all, proceeded to the door of Rani's club. A stocky guy tried the doors and found them locked. He turned to hulking gunners on his flank and nodded curtly.

Three gorillas put their shoulders into it. When the latch gave way, they tumbled in on top of one another, second-rankers crowding close behind.

In another instant they were gone, the portals slamming shut behind them. Bolan made his move. He had come to speak with Rani, and he would not permit the enemy soldiers to divert him from his course.

Bolan crossed the narrow street, his silenced pistol drawn and set for semiautomatic fire. He was a gliding shadow, black death closing in across the open no-man's-land. Neither of the drivers saw him coming as he closed the gap.

There was no question of sparing them, of taking prisoners. They were gunbearers, plain and simple. By their presence, they had doomed themselves to die.

Twenty feet from target, Bolan took the nearer driver with a single, silent parabellum through the ear. The gunner had been talking, but he never finished his sentence. His partner caught a spray of blood and brains. The guncock was momentarily blinded, backpedaling and groping underneath his coat for a weapon he could not reach.

Another gentle squeeze and the Beretta coughed a second time, dispatching another shocker into flesh and bone. The gunner's face caved in, and he died without a sound.

Bolan vaulted over him, closing on the tavern. He holstered the Beretta and dropped the Uzi off its shoulder sling, double-checking the safety. When he hit the double doors, the little chattergun was ready for all comers.

Inside, the soldiers were advancing on the corridor that led to Rani's office, overturning chairs and tables en route. Bolan's explosive entrance took them by surprise and brought them spinning into confrontation with the unexpected menace, several of them peeling off to either side and seeking cover. Hungry guns were tracking onto target acquisition, some of them already sending out probing fire in his direction.

Bolan caught a pair of gunners, hitting them with a rising spiral burst of parabellum manglers. Flesh and bone and fabric sprayed off in all directions, as the gunners fell in a crumpled heap.

Survivors were finding the range. Bolan threw himself into a diving shoulder roll. He scattered tables and came to rest behind one, the Uzi out and probing for another human target. The enemy was searching for him; bullets chewed up his meager shield. He could hold his ground another moment, then. . . .

A soldier broke from cover on his right and rushed his position. The scum was armed with a Skorpion machine pistol, laying down a deadly cover fire, advancing on the run.

Bolan held the Uzi's trigger down and cut the gunner's legs from under him. A ragged scream was severed as he fell across the line of fire, and Bolan's parabellums punched him over in an awkward, lifeless sprawl. Momentum carried him another dozen paces, bodysurfing on a slick of blood.

The Uzi emptied and Bolan ditched the useless magazine, reloading on the move. He snaked across the grimy tile, sighting on the hostile muzzle-blasts and answering with short precision bursts. One of his enemies was silenced, then another and another, slowly whittling the odds against survival.

Behind the bar, a rifleman was sniping at him with a folding-stock Kalashnikov. Bolan snapped a burst at the bastard, but the heavy bar absorbed the parabellum rounds and left his enemy intact.

The Executioner sprang a frag grenade from his web belt, dodging as he freed the pin and dropped the spoon. A looping overhand sent the grenade behind the bar. A miniature volcano erupted, spewing out the rifleman in tattered bits and pieces. Bolan huddled underneath the rain of flesh and shrapnel, battered by the heavy-metal thunder of the blast.

A ringing stillness fell across the smoky killing ground. No one was firing on him; he had the field to himself.

There was no sign of Rani in the tavern. Bolan knew the tavern keeper would have gone to ground when the killing started. . . if he was inside the club at all. The Executioner knew he would have to rout him out quickly.

Bolan scrambled to his feet and cautiously made his way across the barroom, homing on the corridor to Rani's private office. There were rooms upstairs, perhaps another exit—too damn many hiding places.

He shouldered through a beaded curtain, let the Uzi lead him down a dimly lighted hallway. At the far end, Rani's office door was standing partly open, beckoning him in silent invitation. Bolan made it in a dozen strides, nudged the door open with a toe and stepped inside.

A sudden rush of air, a snarling, and the world collapsed on top of him.

A massive fist impacted on Bolan's temple, sending him sprawling, his Uzi skittering across the floor. A roaring, savage scream, scarcely human, drowned the ringing in his ears.

Bolan met the desk head-on, rebounded, fighting to regain his balance. He pivoted, recognized Rani's bodyguard, Amal, before the guy collided with him, driving him back against the desk. His one arm was pinned by the bear-hugging bastard, and he was unable to reach the Beretta. For an instant they were face to face. Bolan studied the enemy's pitted cheeks—a tiny lunar landscape carved in flesh—with the ugly scar slashed across one side.

The giant's grip was crushing him, and the Executioner felt his short ribs grating on each other, sending bolts of agony along his spine. The blood was roaring in his ears, and he remembered the warning signals of impending blackout. Another moment, and he would be helpless, at the Tuareg's mercy.

It was now or never.

Bolan brought his free hand up and over, fingers reaching for the giant's eyes. Scarface saw it coming and reacted swiftly, wrenching his head away. Bolan missed his target, but sank his thumb into a flaring nostril. With a final, desperate surge of strength, he twisted and was rewarded by an ugly ripping sound.

Scarface shrieked, thrusting Bolan powerfully away. The new momentum magnified his strength, and Bolan ripped his thumb free, releasing a bloody geyser as he slumped against the desk. In front of him, the Tuareg shook himself, clutching a bloody flab of mangled nose and cheek—then he attacked again.

Bolan tried to sidestep the attack, fading left, but Amal clotheslined him, one arm catching him across the chest, slamming him against the massive desk.

Bolan rolled back across the desk and brought his legs up, knees and heels together, muscles coiled like springs of steel. He lashed out, catching his adversary in the chest, driving him backward. For an instant, the bodycock was shaken, out of breath, and then a slim stiletto blossomed in his fist.

Bolan's right hand found the holstered Auto-Mag and wrenched it free of leather. The Tuareg was closing on him and he squeezed off, closing the gap with 240 grains of lethal thunder.

And the giant's face was changing, folding, imploding. The force of impact lifted him off his feet and drove him backward. He was airborne when the second .44 slug took him underneath the chin and vaporized his skull.

The headless mannequin collided with a cabinet and rebounded in a sprawl. Bolan was recovering his balance when the cabinet began to move, revolving outward to reveal a yawning tunnel.

Bolan saw it all: Rani making preparations for a hasty getaway, sacrificing Scarface to protect his butt, the claustrophobic journey underground. The tavern keeper had a lead, but maybe there was still a chance of overtaking him.

Bolan shook himself, discarding pain and

weariness, then recovered the Uzi. Precious time was running out.

The Executioner was going underground.

Darkness swallowed him. He marked the bats and scuttling rodents, noxious sewer sounds and smells. The pencil flash revealed his course and kept him going. Light from Rani's office faded, disappeared behind him; he could almost feel the walls closing in.

The ground began to rise as the rathole wound toward a terminus. A faint illumination beckoned him. Bolan pocketed the flashlight, homing on the beacon as it grew and brightened into the outline of a door. In another moment, he stood at the threshold, poised to enter, listening.

There were sounds of struggle on the other side, a muffled, familiar voice bawling for mercy. Bolan listened for another voice, some way to estimate the hostile numbers, but his enemies were silently going about their business.

He had located Rani, and the guy was not alone. From the sound of it, the tavern keeper was quickly running out of time.

Bolan scrutinized the door, figuring it was a carbon copy of one in Rani's office. He tested it and felt it move. He then held the Uzi ready as he put his weight behind a powerful shove. Bolan shouldered through, his weapon up and tracking, eyes narrowed against the sudden brilliant light.

The room was out of the writings of the Marquis de Sade, complete with every sort of torture implement imaginable. Bolan took a quick scan of the scene: Rani, battered, bleeding from a ragged scalp wound, was grappling with a pair of black Goliaths decked out in harem garb. He was keeping them busy, but the crushing blows they landed in a steady rain on his head and shoulders were dampening the little man's opposition.

Bolan's unexpected entry drew attention away from the human punching bag. One of the giants growled and rushed him, head down, a lumbering juggernaut. Bolan stroked the Uzi's trigger, rattling off half a dozen parabellum manglers at a range of twenty paces, and the rush became a lifeless slide to nowhere. Momentum carried him along the concrete floor, into a wall.

The other Goliath had come unglued and was shaking Rani in his grasp the way a terrier shakes a rat. From the sash around his waist, he drew an evil-looking khukri dagger and plunged the blade into his captive's abdomen.

Rani screamed and doubled over as the blade was twisted and withdrawn. He was holding his vitals, bloody fingers clasped across the gaping wound, and by the time he reached his knees the giant stood above him, poised and ready for a swift decapitating blow.

Bolan held the Uzi's trigger down and let the stubby man-shredder empty out at 750 rounds per minute. His target was disintegrating, steel-jacket parabellums separating flesh and bone. The hardguy's turban was in orbit, taking half the skull with it, and the blow he aimed at Rani never fell.

Bolan fed the little chattergun another magazine and moved to kneel beside the dying Arab. Through a haze of blood and pain, his eyes fading in and out of focus, Rani could still recognize Bolan.

"I need to find the woman," Bolan told him.

Rani half turned to face the Executioner, and the effort cost most of what he had left. "Woman," the dying man repeated dully.

The Executioner was running out of time. "It's over, Rani. Look around. Your friends have done this to you." Bolan forged ahead relentlessly. "You're dying, dammit. Take the bastards with you."

Something clicked behind the eyes, but it took another moment for the voice to surface.

"El-Biar," he croaked. "The countess."

The title was a mystery to Bolan, but he recognized the address.

In front of him, Rani stiffened, screwing up his face against the sudden pain. When he died, a silent shudder racked his body, and he toppled forward. Bolan caught him, easing his dead weight down into a prone position. Bolan left him there.

El-Biar. The countess.

It was a feeble lead, but it was all he had. The blitz had come full circle, and he had a single stop remaining. It was time to play his final card and raise the ante to its limit.

16

Armand Dusault killed a man for the first time at age fourteen. His victim was a Jewish pawnbroker in Marseilles, a Holocaust survivor who had shunned the lure of Israel, refusing to leave his native France. Armand cared nothing for the old man's religion or his politics. He knew the merchant closed his shop at the same time every day and carried his cash home for safe deposit underneath a mattress. The old man did not believe in banks.

One evening as he started home, Armand was waiting for him in an alley. The Corsican fell in behind his target, slipped an eight-inch carving knife between his ribs and stripped his victim of all valuables. Almost as an afterthought, he cut the pawnbroker's throat from ear to ear.

With the money taken from the corpse, he fed himself and bought a small supply of heroin. The profits were tremendous. He invested widely and diversified in time, alert to any opportunity for personal advancement. There were other murders, brutal lessons to his enemies and weak associates. Along the waterfront, Armand became a force to reckon with.

And the Corsican was learning as he grew. His elders in the underworld could recognize a rising talent, and they sheltered him, provided him with valuable instruction. In time, Armand became a trusted aide to Monzoor Rudolfi, rubbing elbows with the criminal elite of southern France. Claude DeChamps. Alex Korvini. Herbert Silvaterri. All of them dead now, executed by that bastard Bolan, *l'Américain formidable*.

In the wake of the Rudolfi massacre, Armand had helped himself to some of Monzoor's secret cash reserves, abandoning the Riviera for a safer climate. Stopping off in Sicily's Agrigento province, he established ties with Don Cafu, the local Mafia leader. They had enjoyed a cautious union, and the Corsican had profited immensely, nailing down a host of vital contacts in Turkey and the Middle East. And once again, a natural intuition had preserved Armand; he had departed for Algiers a month before that *sacre* Bolan had returned to bury Don Cafu beneath the smoking ruins of his empire.

Algeria had been the smartest move in a career distinguished by incisive tactical decisions. Armand had learned the flesh-trade basics from Monzoor Rudolfi, strengthened his connections in the months with Don Cafu at Agrigento. Minimal expense and muscle put him into business; ruthlessness and cunning allowed him to dominate the field within eighteen months. Competitors were absorbed or liquidated in a brisk and brutal war of acquisition.

The Corsican became a man of power and respect, surpassing even Tom Rudolfi in wealth and influence. Life was good, the future bright . . . until that afternoon.

The winds of change were whipping through Algiers, and several of Armand's associates had been blown away. Survivors, shaken by the sudden stormy violence, were hounding him for aid, demanding swift solutions to the common problem, but Armand was concentrating on survival.

The Corsican was plugging leaks and settling accounts. He had dispatched a crew to punish Rani for the Orient fiasco, and that was only the beginning. Others would experience his wrath before the desert sun rose on another day. It was a time for cleaning house and separating wheat from chaff.

But first, Armand would have to save himself. The enemy was breathing down his neck, endangering his empire and his life. Police and politicians, terrorists and underworld associates were crowding him, declaring that a *capo* who could not protect his friends was useless, expendable. In time the boldest of them would try to rise against him, sensing weakness.

It was time for friends and enemies alike to see his strength.

The Corsican was not alone, but up to now his closest allies had failed to give him cause for confidence. Mustaffa was a weakling, born to privilege, grown soft in the pursuit of fleshly pleasures. And the countess...she was something else entirely. She had shown initiative in capturing the spy—and she had put them all in jeopardy by keeping it a secret, holding onto the captive for her own perverted pleasures and amusement.

Later, when he had the time to spare, Armand would chastise her for that.

At least he had the hostage now, securely under wraps along with all the merchandise he had intended for the evening shipment. When he had the time to question her, she might reveal the secret of his sudden problems.

No, the Corsican corrected himself, she *would* reveal the secret. And she would pray for the release of death before he finished with her.

But the questioning, however vital, would have to be postponed. He had reached a grim decision on his own. Armand was laying down the law.

The triumvirate sat in Armand's study, the Corsican behind a massive desk, the others in padded leather chairs facing him.

As he spoke, Armand watched them intently,

gauging their reactions. Testing them. "It is time to reevaluate our situation," he proclaimed. "Desperate times require decisive action."

The briefest pause, to let their natural anticipation mount, and then Dusault continued. "We are under siege by faceless enemies, beset on every side. Until we can determine who is launching this attack, I have decided to withdraw."

"Withdraw?" Mustaffa seemed confused. "I do not understand."

The countess, Ilse Brunow, made a sour face. "Armand—"

"Be silent," he snapped at her. "If it wasn't for you, we might already know the name of our opposition. Through your dalliance, they gained a precious foothold."

Mustaffa shifted in his chair, leather groaning under him. His voice was cautious as he came to Ilse's aid. "There was trouble here before she found the woman."

"Of course," Armand scolded. "A probe, some warning shots. *Nothing* like this evening's carnage. *Nothing* like the rampage of this shadow warrior as he seeks our uninvited guest."

Mustaffa cleared his throat and began a thorough study of his fingernails. The countess turned a deeper shade of red, but wisely held her tongue.

"We are retiring from the field," Dusault informed them. "Let the duly constituted officers of law and order cope with violence in the streets. If we are not at hand, we cannot share the blame for anything that happens.''

The meaty Arab stiffened and looked at him aghast. ''The business. . . .''

''Will be amply guarded. Soldiers are expendable. Generals are not.''

''Where do you suggest we go?'' the countess asked.

''On a cruise,'' he said. ''My yacht is standing by with full provisions at the Sidi Fredj marina. We will take the company helicopter. . . to avoid potential traffic hazards.''

''And the merchandise?'' Mustaffa prodded.

''It will follow us by truck. Once at sea, we can dispose of any problems at our leisure.''

The Arab seemed about to protest, but he reconsidered. Clearly shaken by the thought of ditching hostages at sea, he kept his reservations to himself. Ilse, on the other hand, was smiling in anticipation. She would watch the show and relish it.

Dusault was growing weary of these two—the flaccid Saudi and his slim, sadistic counterpart. Their support had been important once, a necessary evil, but today the Corsican could stand alone. Instead of just observing burial at sea, he might allow them to participate.

As corpses.

The Corsican stood up, circling the massive

desk. "It's time to go," he said. "I have the pilot waiting outside."

"A moment now," the countess challenged. "I believe—"

She never had a chance to finish her sentence. Outside, a powerful explosion tore the night apart, its shock wave rattling the study windows. The initial blast was followed by another and another, rapid-fire detonations marching toward the house like the footsteps of an angry giant.

Sudden panic gripped the Corsican with sickening intensity. It took a will of iron to keep his features blank, prevent his voice from cracking when he spoke. "The helicopter—hurry," he commanded. "We are out of time."

Ilse and the Arab both recovered quickly from their momentary shock, and they were moving out as ordered, wasting no more time on questions. Watching them, Dusault was thankful for their survival reflexes. In spite of quirks and weaknesses, they each responded with alacrity to danger.

The Corsican delayed a moment, found the automatic pistol in his desk and slipped it into a pocket. With the enemy upon him, he would not rely entirely on his palace guard for safety.

Even generals have to stand alone at times.

Prepared for anything but failure, he left the lavish study, following Mustaffa and the countess. Somewhere out in the darkness, enemies were waiting for him, but the thought of death held little terror now. He had existed in its shadow from his childhood, grown accustomed to the shade.

A creature of the twilight shadows, he would be at home in darkness, even though his enemies sought sanctuary there. Committed to survival, he would track them down and kill them all before he let the work of a lifetime slip through his fingers.

Armand Dusault was going out to meet the enemy and show them what a man could do. He was going out fighting, and he would recognize no substitute for victory.

It was a battle to the death, and suddenly the Corsican felt right at home.

17

Crouching on the darkened hillside, Bolan scanned the manor house and grounds below. Floodlights were burning around the Corsican's château, lighting up foot patrols with automatic weapons and an executive chopper waiting on a helipad out back. Infrared Nitefinder goggles helped him pick out other sentries on the dark perimeter, teams of two and three circulating randomly among the trees.

Bolan was in blacksuit, face and hands darkened with combat pigments. The AutoMag and Beretta occupied their honored places, web belt heavy with the weight of extra magazines and hand grenades. He wore the lethal Uzi slung across his back, but the little stuttergun was in reserve.

As his hand weapon, Bolan had selected the deadly XM-18 projectile launcher. It had already served him in the early stages of his Casbah blitz, and he was counting on the portable artillery to give him the edge he needed now.

Made of cast aluminum and coated steel, the

launcher weighed sixteen pounds, and resem-
bled an inflated version of the classic Thompson
submachine gun. The drum-style magazine contained a dozen 40mm rounds in any combina-
tion of the gunner's choice, and the weapon
operated much like a revolver. If the weapon
was in the semiautomatic mode, a practiced
hand could empty the drum in five seconds flat.
The stubby gun's rifled barrel gave a marksman
extraordinary accuracy with a choice of high-
explosive or incendiary rounds, gas or smoke,
lethal buckshot or fleshette.

Double belts of alternating rounds were
strapped across the warrior's chest, and he had
primed the launcher with a deadly mix of HE,
gas and fleshette cannisters for his initial strike.

Bolan started down the terraced slope. He
passed undetected by a pair of gunners. He
could have taken them at any time, a swift and
silent double punch with the Beretta, but he let
them go. Any confrontation had its risks, and
he was saving everything for the main event.

At a hundred yards, he was well within the
launcher's maximum effective range, but Bolan
was after pinpoint accuracy. With captives
hanging in the balance, hidden somewhere on
the premises, nothing less would do.

Another team of gunners was approaching in
the darkness, and Bolan found cover in the
shadows, allowing them to pass. They were

close to the nightfighter, conversing in a kind of bastard Arabic sprinkled with French, and both were carrying Beretta Model 12 submachine guns.

The troops were armed but far from ready. Cautious soldiers might have spotted him, would certainly have checked the undergrowth along their beat, but these men were casual, too relaxed. If all of them were equally negligent about their duties, Bolan's job would be a good deal easier.

The trees thinned out around him, clearing completely at a range of sixty yards from target. Open lawn stretched before him, sloping gently to the broad veranda and the house beyond. From where he stood in the shadows, Bolan had a good view of the house. In front of it was a curving drive with several cars lined up. On his left stood a smaller guesthouse or perhaps the servants' quarters. The helipad and waiting chopper were between the buildings, with a pair of flankers in attendance, standing watch.

Bolan wanted to announce his arrival, get the enemy's attention. That was easy—he could ring the doorbell with a high-explosive round.

Bolan primed the launcher, swiveled toward the manor house and set his sights on a limousine, the first car in line. Recoil from the XM-18 was minimal; a steady hand on the launcher's forward pistol grip would hold the weapon on target, even during rapid fire. A skillful gunner could stand off an army with the stubby silver cannon.

He squeezed off, held the weapon level, tracking onto the second target. His first HE round impacted on the lead car's nose and detonated into rolling thunder. The limousine reared up, its hood a piece of airborne shrapnel. A ball of oily flame devoured the front half of the car. Gasoline was spilling from the ruptured tank, igniting as it hit the ground. In another second the fuel reserve erupted in a stunning secondary blast.

The Executioner's first four rounds were high-explosive cans, and Bolan squeezed them off in a rapid succession, a marching line of thunderbolts devouring the cars, consigning them to hell. Gas tanks followed, exploding like a giant string of fireworks.

Sentries were responding, racing to the scene. Bolan let them reach the cars and collect around the pyre before he opened fire again. Troops who attempted to bring order out of chaos had no chance.

The eight remaining tubes of Bolan's launcher held an alternating mix of CS gas and fleshette rounds. The soldier gave himself an angle and let it rip, tracking left to right and back again, bringing down the curtain on their fireside convocation.

Downrange, the hostile troops were enveloped in a rolling, gagging cloud of gas. Before they could recover, the razor-edged fleshettes were ripping into flesh and fabric, riddling the gunners where they stood. Shrieks of pain and terror sounded as they toppled, writhing, to the ground.

It had taken only seven seconds to destroy the first detachment. Bolan paused, reloading. The twist of a lever broke his launcher at the breach, the drum rotating outward to eject spent casings and receive replacement rounds. The ammo in his bandoliers was ready to reload by touch, without a conscious effort on the soldier's part. By the time another squad of gunners showed themselves, the Executioner was ready, racing for the house.

On his right, a clutch of hardmen had him spotted, riot guns and rifles tracking onto target. Bolan went into a crouch, dispatching a high-explosive round in their direction, scattering the enemy like rag dolls in a hurricane. Before the last of them touched down, the Executioner was in motion once again, homing on his target.

To his left, a pair of hostile flankers stood their ground, laying down a probing fire from short Beretta stutterguns. Bolan hit them with a booming fleshette round at twenty yards and watched them come apart on impact, shredded by the storm of whistling darts. He put them out of mind before they hit the turf, already moving out of there and into other confrontations.

Closing on the house, the warrior turned his back on burning cars and broken bodies. Firing on the run, he punched a smoke can through a downstairs window and followed quickly with a round of choking CS gas. Confusion was the ticket. He would let his enemies experience the panic of impending holocaust before they met the grim reality.

A brace of gunners was emerging from the double doors in front when Bolan got there. He swept them off the porch with a blizzard of fleshettes and kept on going.

IN THE DARKENED GUESTHOUSE, Smiley Dublin huddled with the other captives. There were seventeen in all, and fewer than a third of them spoke any English.

Earlier, when they were thrown together, Smiley had attempted conversation but the women were withdrawn and frightened. Several of them drifted in and out of consciousness, minds befuddled by the drugs their captors used to keep them docile.

Smiley stood, stretching, trying to ignore the pain of scrapes and bruises. All her wounds were superficial, but the pain had been excruciating, out of proportion to the damage, and the memory of it lingered in her aching muscles, tender flesh. When she thought about her hours spent in the basement with that bitch—the one they called the countess—Smiley felt a rush of color rising in her cheeks. Cruel humiliation overshadowed pain as she recalled her grim inquisitor—the purring voice and probing, hurting hands.

Smiley had survived that brutal, sadistic torture only by releasing her mind from her pained body. As the countess indulged in her sick fantasies, the tough female Fed dreamed of freedom, of revenge and of her savior, Mack Bolan.

She conjured up a clear vision of Mack, dressed in the traditional threads of U.S. mercenaries, armed to the teeth, protecting her with mighty firepower. And Smiley pictured herself wearing the wardrobe of a belly dancer, the halter top clinging tightly to her breasts—it was the last outfit she had seen a free woman wearing, and it became hers.

In the freedom dream of Smiley Dublin, she and the Executioner were escaping the hell of Algiers, making a getaway through the violence-racked streets of the Casbah. Freedom seemed but a corner away, and Smiley longed to turn that corner, turn it with Mack.

Reality—the screaming voice of the countess—soon brought Smiley's mind back into her body, and with pain shooting through her

limbs, she made a vow to herself: she would
not be sold for slaughter. She would fight,
and she would win. She would destroy the
countess.

Smiley shook herself into the present. They
were under guard inside the little three-room
structure, a pair of gunners at the front and at
least one at the back. From her place near the
windows, she could hear them talking, moving.
On the way in, she had noted that they carried
semiautomatic side arms. One of them, un-
doubtedly the leader of the detail, was armed
with a stubby submachine gun.

There *had* to be a way out, she thought. It
only took some planning, some teamwork.

Smiley turned to face the other women, moving closer, lowering her voice to a whisper. She
concentrated on the English speakers, hoping
some of the others would go along on instinct
when it came time to move.

"We have a chance," she said, projecting
confidence. "They have to come inside for us,
sooner or later. When they do, we can surprise
them, take their guns away."

A murmur rippled through the group, a sharp
exchange of worried glances. One of the women
turned to a companion, whispered rapidly in
French, and the companion blanched, shook her
head in an emphatic negative. In the front row,
a slender British woman spoke up.

"How can we overpower them? They're armed."

"We use the advantage of surprise," Smiley told her. "We've already got the numbers. Hell, it's six to one for our side."

"Assuming that we only meet the three we've seen."

Smiley shook her head. "Assuming nothing. Four guns between us would provide an edge. We could find the perimeter, be out of here before the main force even knows we're gone."

The British woman was thinking, weighing odds and angles. "It's what you Yanks would call a long shot," she said at last. She was smiling. "I'm with you then," she added.

With an effort, Smiley kept herself from crowing. She let the sudden rush of pure exhilaration stoke her fire. "That's great," she said, beaming. "I'm Smiley. You?"

"Judy Withers."

She was on a roll now. Turning to the others, she prodded. "All right, who else is with us? Which of you is tired of waiting in the dark to die?"

"What makes you think they plan to kill us?" asked a brunette, whose accent was strictly lower Bronx.

"Put it all together," Smiley told her bluntly. "This time yesterday, they planned to sell you like a piece of meat. The deal fell through. Now, you're nothing but a walking, talking liability."

"It doesn't matter, anyway," a blonde chimed in. There was a touch of Paris in her voice. "Better dead than auctioned off like sheep for slaughter."

"That's right." The gutsy Fed held out her hand. "Smiley Dublin."

Her newfound ally took the hand and pressed it warmly. "Renée DuBois."

"Okay. Any others? Who wants to take some misery out of their stinking hides?"

Hands were going up around the group, tentative at first, then with greater self-assurance. Smiley counted half a dozen new recruits among them, but the others were uneasy, undecided. Several of them turned away from her, embarrassed by their fear; others seemed unsure of what was happening, confused by sedatives or hampered by the language barrier. She could only hope that some of them would go along when the action started.

She took a final hand count. There were nine—exactly half their number was ready to fight back. If they got the chance.

Minutes crept by, each dragging like an hour in purgatory, and they waited. They were at fifteen minutes and counting when Smiley heard the scuff of boots on the porch. Someone in the yard was issuing instructions to the gunners on the porch, and they were answering.

Another moment, and the man with the stutter-gun was in the doorway, his flanker crowding close behind. Smiley and her troop of volunteers were on their feet to greet them.

"*Allez, allez,*" the honcho barked, motioning toward the doorway with his weapon.

Smiley was about to make her move when sudden thunder tore the night apart. Reflected firelight bathed their captors, and the loud explosions were continuing in rapid fire, distracting both sentries for a crucial second.

Smiley attacked the nearest jailer, the edge of one hand batting down his chopper while the rigid fingers of her other found his eyes. The gunner bellowed, his trigger finger clenching in a spasm of pain. The burp gun stuttered, spat a line of manglers directly at his slim companion.

The second gunner was driven backward through the door. Renée and Judy pounced on his bloody form, wrestling with the holstered pistol. Smiley left them to it, pivoted and drove a knee into the groin of the surviving sentry. With a strangled scream, he went down, Smiley and the others on top of him.

Smiley drove a heel into his windpipe, and the fight left him. The guy was occupied with dying, and he gave no resistance when Smiley relieved him of his submachine gun. She dug an extra magazine out of an inside pocket, and other eager hands found the automatic pistol slung beneath his arm.

Smiley gained the porch in time to see a third guard loping into view, his pistol out and searching for a target. She never gave him time to find one, leveling the little burper from her waist and squeezing off a burst that zippered him from crotch to throat. The guy went down and stayed there, twitching in his death throes.

Another kill. Another weapon for her troop of volunteers.

She ducked back inside the guesthouse and listened to the sounds of battle outside. She had a pretty fair idea of what was coming down, and she was anxious to become a part of it.

"Coast is clear—make for the trees," she told the women. "And keep on going. The police are bound to hear the fireworks soon."

"You will come with us?" Renée asked.

"Sorry." Smiley shook her head. "I've still got business here."

And it was far from over. The bravest man she knew was out there somewhere, slaying dragons. Smiley had to back him up in any way she could.

Granted, there were personal considerations. She wanted to be in at the finish, helping Bolan bring the curtain down on the animals. Especially one female animal.

The countess.

Smiley double-checked her submachine gun, thrust the extra magazine into her waistband. She was ready.

She saw the other captives out of the grounds and covered their escape. By the time they made the darkened tree line, she was anxious to be gone and into battle. She spied a bobbing, weaving figure dressed in black, pursued by gunners as he disappeared around the house.

And she was running after him, the little chopper held across her chest, hot blood pounding in her ears, drowning out the noise of battle.

SMOKE AND THE CHOKING FUMES of noxious gas were everywhere. Armand was getting worried, but he did not show it as he steered his two companions down the dark north-south corridor, keeping close, navigating by his sense of touch. He knew the entrance to the dining room should be along there somewhere....

He found the door, opened it and was rewarded by a gust of smoke and gas. His eyes were swollen, blurred with tears, and he could scarcely breathe. The Corsican steered Mustaffa and the countess through the door and fell into step behind them, herding them toward the sliding doors.

Outside, the sounds of battle had increased on every side. An army was attacking. The night was perilous, alive with muzzle-flashes and the hum of angry bullets. They would have to run a gauntlet to the helicopter, where his gunners were standing watch.

If they could make it, they were home free.

"Go on," he snapped, the pistol in his hand, gesturing in the direction of the chopper. The countess broke from cover, pounding toward the helipad without a backward glance. Mustaffa huddled back against the wall, resembling a cornered animal.

"I can't," he blubbered, cringing. Fear and misery were written on his face, and Dusault regarded him with contempt.

"Then stay."

He raised the automatic, sighting quickly, squeezing off. His first round struck the Saudi just above his right eye and punched through, spewing blood and bits of brain on the wall behind him. A second shot impacted on his chin, disintegrating teeth and jaw, before the body tumbled into awkward death.

Another explosion rocked the house—this one from *inside*. Armand followed Ilse, running beneath the floodlights. Another detonation and the lights were gone, extinguished. He was sprinting through the darkness, praying that his eyes would soon adjust.

A line of bullets stitched across his path, chewing up the turf, and Armand veered away, changing course in midstride. The helicopter was almost within his reach, but he could lose it all at any moment.

His heart was pounding when he reached the chopper, shouldering past a guard into the open loading bay. Inside, he found Ilse Brunow huddled in the rear. Armand felt a sudden urge to kill her as he had the Saudi.

But he had no time as part of his château erupted into flames, black smoke pouring skyward in an inky column. He slapped his pilot on the shoulder, flashed a thumbs-up take-off signal as he found a seat, and grappled with the seat belt.

The rotors were in motion, growling, gathering momentum. The helicopter trembled as the engines revved. Armand experienced the elevator-ride sensation that preceded lift-off.

They had made it. He could feel the chopper stirring, rising off the helipad.

The Corsican was laughing, loving every second of it, when the world exploded under him, plunging him into fiery darkness.

18

The cannisters of smoke and gas had done their work inside the darkened manor house. A gray fog had filled the ground floor, curling in and out of open rooms, collecting in the spacious central corridor. Armand's men had been in a panic, racing around blindly, without direction, choking.

Mack Bolan had moved among them, spotting the enemy through Nitefinders before they had a chance to notice him. Avoiding confrontation where possible, the Executioner had searched for a special group of targets, faces he had seen that morning through a twenty-power scope.

A jowly Arab.

A hawk-faced woman.

And Armand, the Corsican.

He was counting on a clean sweep, and nothing less would satisfy. If even one of the bastards escaped, they would carry the malignancy abroad, allow the poison tendrils to fan out, take root in healthy soil.

The Executioner was not about to let that happen. He would purge the evil, root and branch, before he quit the field of battle.

The foyer opened into a large living room with a host of other rooms on either side, a curving staircase ahead. On his left, a rifleman stormed out of nowhere, swinging his Kalashnikov into alignment.

The Executioner responded instinctively to the threat, swinging his XM-18 around to meet the charging gunner. He stroked the trigger and held the launcher steady as a spray of razor-sharp fleshettes erupted from the muzzle. In front of him the hollow man was vaporized on impact. Scarlet mist mingled with the man-made fog, and blood streaked the parlor walls.

Bolan spun and was already moving out when automatic weapons started yapping at him from the staircase. Crouching gunners were feeling for the range with squat Beretta submachine guns. In another moment they would have him.

Bolan sidestepped, swinging the launcher up. He triggered three quick blasts in rapid fire. The explosive rounds devoured men, spraying shrapnel in a rain of flesh and wood and shattered plaster.

The battered staircase was groaning, sagging. It finally collapsed into dusty rubble. Any gunners left upstairs would have to find another exit. Conversely, if his prey was on the second floor, the Executioner would have to find a different means of access.

He crossed the living room with long strides and struck off down the central corridor, the XM-18 probing out ahead of him to answer any challenge.

Bolan reached a doorway on his right, shouldered through and found himself inside a lavish dining room. Massive sliding doors were standing open at the opposite wall, and a draft had helped clear the smoke and gas.

The Executioner experienced a sudden sense of déjà vu. He had reconned this room before, from the *outside*, but on that occasion he had been looking through the sliding doors and windows with a sniperscope. The perspective was now different, but the warrior had his bearings.

He heard the sound of chopper engines winding up outside the open doors, large rotors slicing air and gaining speed. There would be scant seconds left until lift-off, and suddenly the pieces fell together in a grim mosaic.

The dragon was about to fly away.

Cursing, Bolan crossed the dining room, upsetting chairs and service carts along the way. He gained the open doors and burst through into the night. The Executioner peripherally registered the lifeless Arab on his right. One dead, two to go.

The savages had had a falling out, it seemed. And someone had done Bolan's job.

Across the lawn, the helicopter was rising from the helipad. The rotor wash was whipping Bolan. Another moment would see them air-borne, rising out of his effective range.

The soldier hit a fighting crouch and held his launcher ready, tightening into the squeeze. There was a crack of smoky thunder as his HE round impacted on the chopper's tail behind the passenger compartment. Smoke and flames were rolling out of the bird. Severed tail rotors sliced through the darkness.

Losing altitude, dropping quickly, the chop-per swung around to face him, both doors flap-ping open, disgorging bodies, loose equipment, anything that was not bolted down. Before the smoke obscured his vision, the Executioner saw the pilot glaring at him through the bubble windscreen. Bolan's launcher belched again, the final round before it emptied out. A cluster of fleshettes exploded in the pilot's face, a storm of shattered glass and tempered steel pinned him to his seat, reducing him to something less than human.

There was no time for reloading. Bolan dropped the empty XM-18 and swung the little Uzi down. Beyond the rolling screen of smoke, he caught a fleeting glimpse of human figures seeking cover.

One of them had to be the Corsican. Another, the woman. To be safe, the Executioner would take them all.

Bolan moved out, submachine gun at the ready. Hunting.

THERE WERE A HUNDRED YARDS of open ground between the guesthouse and the manor. Smiley Dublin had covered half the distance safely, confident that Bolan's strike was drawing off the opposition, when a pair of sentries had spotted her and veered to intercept.

Probing Kalashnikov rounds were whistling past. Smiley had hit a prone position, swung her short Beretta submachine gun toward the sprinting figures and squeezed the trigger.

Half a dozen parabellums had struck the gunner on her right and punched him over backward. The guy's companion had made another dozen yards before she swiveled into target acquisition. A rifle bullet had burned along her flank, another clipped a lock of hair beside her face.

Smiley held the trigger down and tracked her moving target, leading him into the stream of parabellum manglers. The impact lifted him off his feet, sending him into an awkward cartwheel, bullets ripping through him, churning flesh and bone into a lifeless pulp.

The Beretta's bolt locked open on an empty

chamber. She dropped the useless magazine and was snugging its replacement into the receiver as she stood up.

She had a single clip—thirty lethal rounds—left. She would have to make them count.

Another fifty yards took her to the manor house. From the house she saw a clutch of running figures clearing the sliding doors to the left, striking off across the wide veranda toward the helipad and waiting chopper. Smiley caught a glimpse of a familiar face—a face that evoked a tremor inside her.

Smoky fog rolled in, and she lost sight of the countess. Smiley still had the helicopter spotted by its running lights. She could meet her quarry there.

The Fed forgot about the house and everyone inside. Bolan was in there, serving up an order of hellfire, and she left him to it. Smiley had her hands full trying to close the back door. She knew she might already be too late.

Around the helicopter, people were dodging, weaving, scrambling for the loading bays. The rotors were in motion, twirling lazily at first, then rapidly accelerating. Flankers armed with automatic weapons ducked beneath the spinning blades.

At forty yards, Smiley dropped to one knee and snapped her weapon up and onto target.

She fired, leaning into the recoil and saw the nearest sentry stagger, stumble, sprawl.

The helicopter shifted, rising gingerly, and Smiley had the bubble windscreen in her sights when the tail section broke away and erupted into fire. Smoke was rolling out across the lawn as the chopper slewed around, and Smiley saw a slender figure tumble out the open hatch.

The countess.

As the smoke closed in, Smiley swiftly calculated a collision course with the escaping woman. Despite the cool night air, she was perspiring, and the taste of bile was in her mouth. Loathing drove her on to intercept the German, cutting off her only avenue of safe retreat.

Smiley was waiting when a pair of running figures cleared the smoke screen, closing rapidly on her position. She did not recognize the man, but he was armed.

She rattled off three rounds in rapid fire, the echoes merging into one report. Her target staggered and was plowed over. The gunner's shoulders hit the turf before his heels touched down. A final tremor, and the guy was gone.

The slender German countess froze in her tracks, then turned toward the sound of gunfire. Her fighting crouch was feral, an instinctive movement, both hands coming up in front of her, fingers curved into claws. Recognition flickered, locked in place as her eyes fastened on Smiley. "So. *Die Amerikanerin.*"

There was menace in the tone, and Smiley felt a chill along her spine, the short hairs rising on her neck. The countess was sadistic hate personified, the venom channeled through her voice. "You have done well to come so far," she said, her tone taking on a mocking quality. "I felt your strength myself."

Smiley felt her stomach turning over, and she swallowed hard to keep the contents down. "It's over," she informed the countess.

Apprehension was quickly lost within the calculating gaze. "Not yet, *liebchen*," she retorted. "Not just yet."

The movement, though anticipated, was so swift and fluid it almost took Smiley by surprise. She saw the German's right hand dipping down and out of sight, returning with a boot knife.

Smiley saw the cold stiletto as it left the enemy's hands, and she could hear its death whisper in the darkness. She was turning, side-stepping, when the knife connected, grazing a breast and burrowing deep into her biceps.

Beneath the shock and sudden pain, abiding fury gripped her soul. Firing one-handed, Smiley held the squat Beretta chopper steady, her anger and disgust erupting from the muzzle in a stream of parabellum manglers. At a range of less than twenty feet, there was no way to miss her target.

Ilse Brunow shrieked and tried to ward off the bullets with outstretched palms. Sizzling steel-jackets drilled through her hands, destroying the screaming face and everything behind it. Twisting, spinning, driven by the force of impact, the countess evaporated where she stood.

The stuttergun was empty, and Smiley let it drop. There was no need to view her handiwork, to verify the kill. Her aim was true, the range point-blank. And it was over.

No.

Not yet.

The sounds of battle close at hand informed her that the strike was still in progress. It was Bolan, up against the odds as always.

Smiley, clutching her wounded arm, moved around the riddled corpse of Ilse Brunow, taking off in search of Bolan and the battle.

THE SMELL OF BURNING FLESH and helicopter fuel enveloped Bolan as he stalked the killing ground, searching for his target. In his hands, the Uzi was a grim extension of himself, still hungry.

Footsteps closed on his flank, and Bolan turned and saw a figure looming in the smoke. A pistol cracked, and he threw himself to one side, diving as the bullet snapped above him.

The Executioner answered with his submachine gun, ripping off a burst before he came to rest, another as he found the prone position. Ten yards away, the human target stumbled through an awkward pirouette and fell.

Bolan waited for twenty seconds, and when the hostile fire was not repeated he stood up and advanced with caution. Sudden stillness cloaked the battlefield, as if surviving soldiers felt the chill of death and sought to hide from its embrace.

Bolan found Armand the Corsican laid out on blood-stained grass, one leg doubled back beneath him, arms outstretched. Blood was leaking from the wounds where parabellum rounds had stitched across his abdomen.

But he was still alive.

The chest was rising, falling, with the effort of his ragged respiration. Glassy eyes shifted toward the Executioner as he approached. The right hand quivered, fingers flexing weakly, but the autoloader was beyond his reach forever.

Armand could see death. His lips moved, struggling to form coherent sound. Bolan studied him closely and then knelt beside him, leaning close to catch the whispered words.

"Nothing changes," he was gasping. "Everything goes on the same."

"You're wrong," the Executioner told him. "For you, it ends right here."

The Corsican was trembling, sudden fury blazing in his eyes. He might have lunged at Bolan, but the ravaged body was not taking any further messages.

The man was dying, and he knew it. Nothing in the world could save him, and the guy was choking on the bitter gall of failure, fading fast. *"You haven't won,"* he grated, but the words were hollow, filled with bitterness.

Bolan pushed the Uzi's muzzle in between the Corsican's lips and silenced further comment.

The Executioner rose, turned and took himself away from there. The viper's head was severed, crushed. The mission was complete—except for Smiley and the hostages.

They would be close at hand, he knew, if they were still alive.

There had been no sign of Smiley in the manor. He would check out the guesthouse.

He was passing the burned-out helicopter when a movement on his left alerted him to danger. Pivoting, he drew the AutoMag and sighted down the vented barrel, making target acquisition at a range of thirty yards. But there was something in the figure's walk, the posture, that made him hold his fire.

Recognition struck him like a fist above the heart, and Bolan sheathed the silver cannon, moving out to meet the wounded lady Fed. They fell together, held each other close.

And for the moment, it was over in Algiers. Amid the stench of death and burning, Bolan smelled a trace of victory.

"YOU HAVEN'T WON. . . ."

The Corsican was right, of course, and Bolan knew it. There was no such thing as final victory in a war that lasts forever. Savage Man knew nothing of surrender, precious little of retreat.

But Bolan had the will to turn him back. A single warrior, ably supported by dedicated allies, he was equally committed to the battle of attrition. Tonight, Bolan had a victory of sorts to celebrate. The flesh markets of Algiers were empty. Tonight, the savages were beaten, driven back into their caves and tunnels, momentarily leaderless. But the Executioner did not deceive himself into thinking he had won a lasting triumph.

The war was everywhere, the foe widespread. For every cannibal dispatched, a dozen seemed to surface. There would be other savages and other struggles, possibly in old Algiers itself.

But not tonight.

Mack Bolan led Smiley Dublin from the field, leaving the battleground to stray survivors. Distant sirens marked the approach of officers and medics.

For now it was over. For now he was free.

Don Pendleton on

MACK BOLAN

Mike Newton is a seasoned author and a battle-tested veteran of the Bolan wars. From his professional debut, in *The Executioner's War Book*, there has been no looking back, and *Sold for Slaughter* represents his forty-fourth book published in the span of seven hectic years.

He's a great writer; do read #41: *The Violent Streets*, #45: *Paramilitary Plot* and #55: *Paradine's Gauntlet* for the best of Mike. A lifelong student of the Mafia and underground subversive movements, he now brings a special expertise to Bolan's clash with slavers in Algiers.

Sexual slavery is as old as man's recorded history. With torture, drugs, intimidation, the commercial flesh-peddlers have terrorized communities, entire societies. In America, a frightened Congress met their depredations with the Mann Act during 1910, and thirty-five years later Lucky Luciano, Boss of Bosses for the New York Mafia, was locked away and finally deported on charges of compulsory prostitution.

Elsewhere, slavers have continued at their savage trade until the present day, and nowhere is their presence felt as strongly as the Middle East and Northern Africa. For Bolan, the matter has the grim imperative of here and now.

The *War Book* will soon be back, by the way, in an entirely new edition that will showcase dramatic developments in Mack Bolan's career. To begin the unfolding of these major events, The Executioner returns to Southeast Asia in #61: *Tiger War*. Look out—this one is an *epic* smash against evil!

Don Pendleton

MACK BOLAN

THE EXECUTIONER 61

appears again in
Tiger War

A trap!

So much for undercover operations, thought Bolan.
His nightmare parachute drop into Thailand had
become an open secret. Enemy gunfire zeroed in on
his position. It was survival time in the jungle again!

The Executioner was in Southeast Asia's Golden
Triangle to strike at the international drug industry. But
his advance man has been captured by the 93rd
Kuomintang Division of the Nationalist Chinese Army.

Now Bolan's Montagnard army refused to fight. The
tribesmen, hereditary enemies of the Chinese for
4,000 years, were fierce warriors yet fickle allies.
They knew better than to back a loser. . . .

But Bolan would not lose. However much death it
took!

JOIN FORCES WITH MACK BOLAN AND HIS NEW COMBAT TEAMS!

Mail this coupon today!